Aunt Fanny

Pop-Guns, One Serious and One Funny

Being the First Book of the Series

Aunt Fanny

Pop-Guns, One Serious and One Funny
Being the First Book of the Series

ISBN/EAN: 9783337021351

Printed in Europe, USA, Canada, Australia, Japan

Cover: Foto ©Andreas Hilbeck / pixelio.de

More available books at **www.hansebooks.com**

POP-GUNS.

ONE SERIOUS AND ONE FUNNY.

LIST OF POP-GUN SERIES.

I.—Pop-Guns.

II.—One Big Pop-Gun.

III.—All Sorts of Pop-Guns.

IV.—Funny Pop-Guns.

V.—Grasshopper Pop-Gun.

VI.—Post-Office Pop-Guns.

The Dogs' Dinner Party.

POP-GUNS.

ONE SERIOUS AND ONE FUNNY.

BEING

THE FIRST BOOK OF THE SERIES.

BY

AUNT FANNY,

AUTHOR OF "NIGHTCAPS," "MITTENS," "PET BOOKS," "WIFE'S STRATAGEM," ETC.

"Shoot folly as it flies."

"I love God and little children."—RICHTER.

NEW YORK:

SHELDON & COMPANY, PUBLISHERS,

498 & 500 BROADWAY.

1865.

C. A. ALVORD, STEREOTYPER.

THIS, AND ALL THE BOOKS OF THE SERIES,

I DEDICATE

TO

THOMAS LINCOLN,

THE SON OF

THAT LOYAL, FEARLESS, HONEST MAN,

THE

PRESIDENT OF THE UNITED STATES.

CONTENTS.

ILLUSTRATIONS.

PREFACE.

In these little books, I have complied
with a request repeatedly expressed to me,
to write stories avowedly for the purpose
of "pointing a moral."

Any one who will take the trouble to
look over the "Nightcap," "Mitten," or
"Sock" books, will see that I have tried
to remember this duty; although I own to
loving children so tenderly, as to adminis-
ter *my* pills, sugar-coated.

Even now, I cannot resist employing the
whimsical mask of an odd title; but my

dear friends, *try my pop-guns*, and if then you are convinced that I have sincerely endeavored to "shoot folly as it flies," pray believe also, that AUNT FANNY well knows that stories called "Pop-Guns," will make quicker and more enduring marks in the loving hearts of her darlings, the children, than twenty folios, written by a thousand times greater authors, with the dry · title of "Moral Lessons for the Young."

NEW YORK, *May*, 1864.

POP-GUNS.

A POP-GUN LETTER FROM AUNT FANNY.

DARLING CHILDREN,—

Last summer, when I was in the country, I met a family of six charming children. As soon as they heard who I was, they did not stop one minute to think about it, but just ran up and kissed and hugged me, and told me they loved me dearly.

Oh! how sweet that was to know: but I put on a funny grave face, and said—

, "I cannot imagine why you should love such a little brown woman: don't you think you have made some mistake?"

"No indeed, Aunt Fanny," they all cried together, "and we are *so* glad we have found you at last. We are glad you are little, that's the best of it! and you don't look so *very* brown. Come, please sit down, and tell us what has become of the Night-cap children, won't you? Oh, do!"

There was no resisting that "Oh, do!" with six pair of loving bright eyes looking into mine; so I answered—

"Well, let us all get in a corner together, and have a nice long talk."

At this one of the boys threw up his hands, made a dry dive down on the carpet, and bumped the top of his head, in his joy; another, hopped on one foot till he lost his balance, and had to make a one-sided somerset, to bring himself up on his feet again; the third and smallest laid his curly head lovingly against my dress; while the little girls danced and skipped so lightly around me, that I caught myself wishing for the hundred and fiftieth time that I were a child too.

But never mind. I love children with

my whole heart, and that helps to comfort me, when I think what an old "Aunt Fanny" I am getting to be.

So we all sat down in the corner, just as close together as we could get, and I told them how, as they knew already from the "Mitten" books, that George was a captain in the army, and as he had always been a good boy, he was now a noble and good young man; and how Harry had gone to the naval school at Newport, and could run about the rigging of a ship, like any monkey; and Anna was engaged to be married; at which they were greatly surprised.

"Why, Aunt Fanny!" they exclaimed, "is she as *old* as that?"

"Yes," I answered, "she *would* grow up into a lovely young lady, all I could do—and the rest are growing older too, for Clara has left school; little Minnie knows how to make cake; the 'TREMENDOUS DOG' has died of old age; and even little

Johnny, who packed up his mother's false hair in an old tin tomato-can, and gave it to the express-man to carry off, is taller than I am."

"Oh, Aunt Fanny! how old they all are!" cried Sophie, the eldest girl, "they are *too* old to have any more stories told to them. Oh! oh!" she exclaimed, clapping her hands, "please tell the next stories to us. Won't you? will you?"

Such a shout as the rest of the children gave at this! "Yes! yes! yes!" they all cried. "We'll be the Night-cap children! we want the next stories! Oh my! how delightful it would be!"

"But let me tell you," I said, with a serious air, "you would not be the *Night-cap* children. I have a new idea in my head. I am going to write stories this time, in which I intend to show the evil effects of special faults and bad habits, and the unfailing happiness children will find in being good, and doing good. Yes, I am

going to fire *guns* this time; and then, if
the stories are first told to you, what *do*
you think you will be called?"

"W-h-a-t?" cried all the children, with
breathless interest.

I put on a monstrous solemn face, and
raising my arms as if I was going to shoot,
uttered the first four words very slowly,
and the last four, very quickly—

"You — will — be — called — THE POP-
GUN CHILDREN — BANG!"

But I could not help a merry twinkle in
my eyes, and the children saw it; so after
the first instant of surprise at their new
and queer title, they burst out into hearty
chuckling laughter, exclaiming, "Oh, what
fun! We are to be the 'Pop-gun Children!' Shoot away, Aunt Fanny. Make
ready! Take aim! Fire! Bang! bang!
bang!" and they commenced to shoot each
other with their fore-fingers, and made
such a terrible racket, that two very grave
and very prim old ladies, who were knit-

ting stockings on the other side of the room, looked at us so severely through their big round spectacles, that I had a great mind to tell the children to take hold of hands, and we would all march up in one long row, and with a One, two, three! fall down plump on our fourteen knees, and say we were sorry for being happy so loud.

But the next moment, I thought, that perhaps these poor old souls had no children in their own homes, and were not used to so much noise—perhaps they had only cats and parrots to love them—and then I felt sorry for them in earnest, and whispered to the children, "Come, let us go out under the trees, and finish our talk."

It would have made you smile, if you could have seen how they tried to get the dimples out of their faces, as they walked past the two old ladies. They puckered their mouths into button-holes, and seemed to be stepping on eggs, but the very instant they got outside the front door I really thought they had wings all at once, for they seemed to fly under a great oaktree, where there was a large rustic seat, and tumbling down pell-mell upon it, Fred, the eldest boy, cried out, "Walk up, ladies and gentlemen! here you will see the celebrated Pop-Gun Children, each a head and five pair of shoulders taller than anybody else, because they have got Aunt Fanny all to themselves: ten cents each, and children half-price, and we intend to give the money to the *in*sanitary commis-. sion."

This made me laugh so, that I did not perceive that a lady and gentleman who had been sitting reading under another tree a little way off, had left their seats, and were standing close to us smiling, until Sophie said, "Dear mamma and papa, this is 'Aunt Fanny.'"

I tried to look grave, as I shook hands

2

with "mamma and papa," and heard their
kind words of welcome: words so kind,
that I do not like to tell them—and then
all the children speaking at once, told
about their new funny name, and my new
stories, at which mamma and papa seemed
very much delighted.

"But when will they begin?" asked the
children; "to-morrow?"

"Not till next October."

"O———h!" now came, in one long
wail of disappointment.

"Why, my darlings," I said, "I want
to rest here in this lovely country place,
and laugh and frolic with you, and climb
over ninety-nine fences, and eat apples,
and drink milk, and hear the birds sing,
and watch the dimples of sunlight peeping
through the leaves of the trees, and feed
the chickens, and ride on the top of a load
of hay, with forty thousand grasshoppers
in it, and sail or row on that beautiful
little lake in front of us, and forget all

"We all got into the boat."

about the hard brick and stone city, until the sweet summer is over."

"Oh! will you do all that with us, dear Aunt Fanny? then we will wait as long as you like. When will you begin to climb the fences and row on the pond? Let's have a row now."

"With all my heart," I said, and we jumped up and ran down to the water's edge; at least the children ran, and I tried to, and we got into a beautiful little boat, and had *such* a nice row, with the cool soft wind blowing in our faces, and the air full of golden light. Oh! it did me more good than a thousand doses of Epsom salts.

The very minute we were on dry land again, Peter said, with a hop, skip, and jump, "Now, Aunt Fanny, when shall we begin to climb the fences?"

"At five o'clock this afternoon," I answered, laughing, "we will all go out, for a nice long walk, and you shall hunt up

the fences, and that little pug-nosed dog,
with no tail to speak of, shall go with us.''

"Why, that's our dog!" cried the children.

"Is it? what is his name?"

"Something short."

"Short? Is it Tip?"

"No, Aunt Fanny; something short."

"Nip? Bip? Rip? Sap? Top?"

How they laughed as they said again,
"Something short."

Then I began to suspect the joke, and
said, "Very well. I'll fire one of my pop-
guns at Mr. Something Short, the very
first time I catch him chasing a cat, or
rushing at cows' noses to bite them."

"Yes do, Aunt Fanny!" they answered.
Then I got a good kiss and hug from each,
and went back into the house.

*   *   *   *   *   *

And here, my darling children who are
out in the world, are the stories I gave,
one by one, to Sophie, Kitty, and Lou;

Fred, the diver; Peter, the hopper; and Bob. *You* have them printed in books; but, oh dear! I cannot see you as I did the others, and watch your sweet faces, to know if you like them. I only wish I *could* get hold of you all, and give you one good kiss apiece. I often have my parlors filled with lovely children, who wish to see "Aunt Fanny." It makes me feel very, very happy; but I keep wanting more to come all the time.

My Pop-gun children seemed really to know "Night-caps," "Mittens," "Socks," and the "Pet-Books" by heart; and I do hope that both they and you who will read these new stories, will make an earnest resolution to profit by the good examples I shall give, and avoid all that you will find to be evil. I don't mean it all for fun. No indeed! To be sure I have given a funny title to the books, and shall try to tell *some* funny stories; but beneath this fun I want you to feel that I am also try-

ing to show you how the cultivation of
high and generous qualities, and noble
and right principles, is the only way by
which you may reap real and steadfast
happiness—the only way to win the love
and respect of all around you.

You know Solomon says, "Even a
child is known by his doings—whether
his work be pure, and whether it be
right;" and you will be more laughing
and merry—more full of fun and frolic at
the right times—more the pictures of almost perfect happiness—the more earnest-
ly you endeavor to obey your parents,
study your Bible, learn your lessons, and,
above all, the more faithfully you say
your prayers. Never, never forget your
prayers, my own darlings; then you will
be certain, if the good God spares your
lives, to grow up good and useful men and
women.

Forgive me for this grave little lecture.
It all came out of LOVE—that best love

which seeks your good. If you love me, I know you will understand this.

And now here are the Pop-gun Stories, which I send with a—Take aim! fire! bang!! and on top of all a kiss and a blessing, from your loving

AUNT FANNY.

ABOUT THE CHILDREN.

ONE clear soft autumn evening, in the beginning of October, just after dinner, Aunt Fanny went up into her bedroom, and put on her bonnet and sack. They were both black, and trimmed with crape, for she had lately lost a relative she dearly loved. Then opening a drawer in her precious little library-table, upon which she wrote all her stories, she took out a manuscript, and tried to get it into her pocket.

But it was written on such wide paper that the end would stick out, so she had to return to the dining-room with a quarter of the roll in full view.

"Why, mamma!" exclaimed Alice, "where are you going? and what is that sticking out of your pocket?"

"I am going to see my new children, and this is the but-end of a pop-gun."

"Oh, mamma, take me! I want to go."

"But, darling, I thought Lizzie Lyman was coming to help you make a new Spanish waist for Ginevra."

"So she is; I forgot;" and Alice pulled out Miss Ginevra, who was a lovely little porcelain doll, and who lived in the top of her own trunk, and kissed her fondly.

So Aunt Fanny and her tall husband, after a dozen kisses or so from Sarah and Alice, trotted off.

If you will promise never to tell, I will mention that the new children lived in Twenty-third street, in the very middle of a long row of brown-stone houses. It was not a very long walk, and soon Aunt Fanny had pulled the bell, which was one of those funny spring bells which give one loud "tching," as if they had jumped out of their skins with a jerk and a scream; and jumped in again with another, the

next time anybody pulled them. As the
door was opened, she saw a bright little
face peeping from the dining-room, and
the very next instant she heard the joyous
exclamation, "If it isn't Aunt Fanny!"—
and then came a rushing, and a tumbling,
and a racing, and a laughing! and all the
six children fell lovingly upon her, and
knocked down—not Aunt Fanny, not a bit
of it, or of her, but two hats, three um-
brellas, a great-coat, a whisk-broom, and
a paper parcel marked "From A. T. Stew-
art,"—all of which had been peacefully
hanging or resting upon the hat-stand;
and when papa and mamma came out to
see who was creating such a riot, there
was Aunt Fanny with the whisk-broom
perched like a flower on top of her bonnet, Peter and Fred rushing after the hats
which had rolled off in different corners;
all the rest of the articles scattered on the
floor; Bob and the three little girls jumping straight up and down, kissing Aunt

Fanny, and begging pardon for upsetting so many things over her; while the waiter and Aunt Fanny's husband were standing near, laughing as hard as ever they could at the fun.

They got into the parlor at last, and sat down—the children with their bright eyes fastened upon their welcome guest, who, trying to look grave, asked, the very first thing, if the children had had any dinner that day.

"Why yes, plenty, Aunt Fanny; dessert too—flower-pot pudding."

"*Flower-pot* pudding! who ever heard of such a pudding! Is it any thing like dirt-pies?"

"Why no, Aunt Fanny!" cried all the children; "it is *cooked* in flower-pots; at any rate, we call them so; but there are no holes in the bottoms of them. Mamma brought ever so many of these funny little brown earthen pots from Boston. The cook puts them in the oven only half full

of the pudding, but when they come out,
oh my! how funny they look! for each
one has swelled up twice as high as the
pot, and some of them hang over on one
side, as if they were perfectly tipsy; and
when you come to cut them, pop! goes the
knife into a great hole inside; and there's
where you must put the sauce, and that
makes them taste so nice! but—why do
you ask?"

Aunt Fanny laughed, and said—

"When you came at me so furiously, I
thought you might have been living on a
slice or two of buttered paper and a teacup
or so of sunbeams to-day, and meant to eat
me up for supper."

"Oh, Aunt Fanny! we love you dearly,
but we wouldn't eat you up for all the
world."

"But what's that sticking out of your
pocket?" asked Sophie, spying the end of
the roll of manuscript, for the first time.

"A Pop-gun. Bang!" she answered,

pulling it out and pointing it at them. "Come, sit down, for I have brought it on purpose to read to you."

With a great many "hushes," and flourishes, and skirmishes, to get the seats on either side of her, Aunt Fanny unrolled her story, and began as follows:

HOW PHILIP BADBOY BECAME PHILIP WISEMAN.

Once up- on a time not so very long ago, there lived a stu- pid, heavy looking boy, na- med Philip, who bore any thing but an agreeable char- acter; for he was naughty, lazy, greedy, and impudent. His companions all hated him, for when he appeared among them after school hours, he was sure to kick their marbles into the middle of the street, knock the little boys' caps over their eyes, twitch balls and kites out of their hands, and set them all fighting and quarrelling.

One amusement in particular gave him great delight. This was to tie a knot in the end of his handkerchief and snap with it at the little boys' legs. I really hope no one reading this has ever made a "snapper." If he has, and if he has gone round snapping other boys' legs, I am sure his face has turned as red as a stick of sealing-wax when he reads these lines, and knows that I call him *a cowardly tormentor*, and no better than Philip.

His whole name was Philip Wiseman, but his companions changed it to Philip Badboy.

His parents tried long and faithfully to improve their wayward child; but no-

thing altered him for the better—indeed,
whippings, and locking him up, only
seemed to make him worse.

Do not imagine for a moment that he
was *happy*. No indeed! He was discon-
tented, fretful, forever wishing that dinner
was ready, and oftentimes hating the sight
of every thing and everybody.

At last, quite wearied out, his father put
him at a celebrated boarding-school in
Sing Sing; but they might better perhaps
have put him in the famous prison at the
same place, for not a single button did
Philip care for lessons or punishment.

At this same school was a bright little
fellow, as full of good-nature, fun, and
mischief as he could hold. He did not always know his lessons, and there really
seemed no end to the monkey tricks he
was constantly playing upon his school-
fellows; but somehow, when he said he
was sorry for his idleness, and his capers,
in his coaxing voice, and trying to keep

back two dimples that would come in his cheeks, neither teachers nor comrades could help forgiving him immediately. Everybody loved little Kriss Luff.

He even tried to make friends with Philip; and one bright summer morning resolved to get him up in time for prayers. When the first bell rang, Kriss went to the sleeping boy's bed, and shaking him well, shouted out: "Come, Lazybones, it's time for you to be learning your A, B, C; Get up! get up!"

Philip only snored louder, and gave a kick with one of his legs, whereupon the little fellow, with a ·tremendous push, tilted him suddenly out on the floor, and then had to run for his life, or he would have got a good thrashing from the angry boy.

Thanks to the upset, Philip was down this morning in time for prayers; but went sound asleep again while on his knees, and his neighbors had to poke and pinch

3

him well, to get him upon his feet, when the morning service was ended.

But you may be certain he managed to keep awake at the breakfast table, where he made up for having a head as empty as a drum, by filling his stomach till he could scarcely breathe. He never stopped for salt or pepper; he did not waste his time talking; and was always the very last one at the table, getting up with his cheeks sticking out like a balloon, from thrusting into his mouth every thing he could catch in a hurry.

During school hours, Master Philip went to sleep again—and the master coming up rapped so loudly and suddenly on the desk, that he jumped half a yard high, exclaiming: "Dear me, how *could* you frighten me so!" while all the boys shouted with laughter.

You may imagine that our friend Philip did not injure himself in the least with studying. He was always wishing that

his slate was a hot buttered pancake, so
he could eat it up, and never see it again;
he would stare at his books as if they
were scarecrows, and the idea of writing
a composition brought the tears in his eyes
quicker than red pepper. The whole of
his pocket-money was spent in buying
tough pastry; little round stale pound-
cakes, with three dead flies and two cur-
rants stuck over the top; some oranges,
green apples, and molasses candy. Not a
suck or a bite did one of his school-fellows ever get, for a greedy boy is *always*
selfish.

At last Dr. Gradus gave up in despair,
and wrote a letter to Philip's father, in-
forming him very frankly that there were
no more brains in his son's head than in a
cocoa-nut; that he would do nothing but
sleep and cram, from morning till night;
that he woke the boys in his dormitory
every night by yelling with the nightmare,
because he had eaten so much at supper;

and that he was very sorry, but Master
Philip must leave the school; and he
advised, that the very best thing to do
with him was to bind him out to a plain
country farmer, where he would *have* to
rise at the first peep of day—and work
hard till sunset.

Philip's father thought long and seriously over this letter—then he took a journey; and on his return he brought with
him a farmer, and an intelligent-looking
country lad.

The boy's name was John Goodfellow,
and he looked as good as his name—
for his clear blue eyes sparkled with
good-nature; his cheeks shone with good
health; and his voice had a tone of
good-breeding, notwithstanding his plain
country dress and manners. I have no
doubt his mother was a good woman,
his father a good man, and we know
the name of all three was Goodfellow—and so much goodness in a bunch,

makes me write about it with extra good-will.

A day or two after the return of Philip's father, a great clumsy farm wagon came lumbering up the avenue of Dr. Gradus's seminary; driving it, was a rough-looking man, and beside him sat a bright-faced boy,—the same man and boy who made their appearance, when Philip's father returned from his journey.

The man got down and rang a tremendous peal upon the bell. The servant thought the President of the United States had arrived, and flew to answer it.

"Does Dr. Great Dust live here?" asked the man.

"How dare you come and tear the house down at this rate?" cried the angry servant, seeing that it was not "grand company." "What do you want, you old bear?"

The old bear, being good-natured, burst out laughing. "Don't spoil your pretty

face," he said, "by getting it into a twist.
When I give a pull, I always give a strong
one; and you must a been greasing of
your bell, for it came out like a shot. Hum!
Now s'pose you tell me if Dr. Great Dust
lives here. I should think he did, by the
one you've kicked up about nothing."

"Well, he does, and what of it?"

"Only I want to see him, and here's a
letter," holding it out.

The woman took the letter and showed
the farmer and his boy into a small room,
while she went up-stairs to the doctor's
study.

There he sat, to be sure, a grave, learned
man, with spectacles perched on his nose,
a great frown in his forehead, rather dirty
wristbands, a pen behind his ear, and
ever so many papers before him, written
as full as they could hold of Latin and
Greek themes, which the larger boys in
the school had sent in for examination.
Of course there was no end of mistakes in

most of them ; and as to Philip's copy, it was just one hodge-podge of farrago and nonsense.

"Oh, that hopeless booby of a boy !" the doctor was exclaiming to himself, as he took up this last paper, when there came a knock at the door.

With the permission to enter, the servant approached, handed the letter, and said that there were two bumpkins down stairs waiting for the answer.

"Show them up," said the doctor.

Then he opened his letter, took out an envelope, read the first, stared, read again, rang the bell, and sent for Philip, first giving the servant an order in a low voice.

In the mean time the rough-looking farmer and the boy, neither of whom deserved to be called bumpkins, came in, and, having bowed as well as they knew how, sat down in a corner.

It was during recess in school hours that all this happened, and our idle friend,

Master Philip, was fast asleep in the
school-room. The rind of an orange, the
cores of several apples, a grammar turned
upside down, and some very sticky paper
that had held candy, lay on the desk. In
the midst of them was Philip's head. His
face was very sticky too, and glued fast to
the extreme end of his nose was a paper
pellet with which Kriss Luff had carefully
ornamented it, to the tittering delight of
half a dozen of his comrades. This and
his sticky face had made it the duty of
every fly in the room to invite each other
to the spot to a mass meeting on business, to
which was added a grand feast, and gym-
nastic exercises; so there they all were,
as lively as you please—standing on their
heads, hanging by one leg, whisking, and
frisking, and eating, and buzzing, and
grumbling, and fighting over the spoils,
like hungry hawks or aldermen.

"Wake up, Master Philip!" cried the
servant, giving him a push. "You're

wanted in the doctor's study, and his face is as long as my arm. I guess he has got bad news for you. What's that on the end of your nose?"

"Bad news," repeated Philip, tearing off the paper pellet. "Was it worth while disturbing my nap for that? Go to Guinea!"

"But you must come—"

"Go to Guinea with your bad news!"

"Well, I will tell the doctor what you say."

This threat started Philip, and grumbling to himself he hurried into the study.

When he entered he saw a boy of his own age, who was now standing up studying with great interest a large map of the United States which hung against the wall, a plain, good-natured looking man, and the doctor, who was handing him a letter.

"Philip," said the doctor, with a very solemn face, "I am sorry to tell you that my letter from your father informs me

that you must leave school immediately:
not to go home," he added, for he saw
the boy's face brightening. "Your father
and mother have just left the country on
important business; where they have gone
is to be kept a secret; and now, as you
are determined not to learn—as you have
made up your mind to grow up an igno-
rant, useless creature—your father has
bound you apprentice to this worthy farmer, whose son takes your place here. If
the good man is pleased with you, he is to
give you a small weekly allowance; but
I warn you beforehand, he will put up
with none of your lazy habits; and if he
finds that you will not obey him, why
then"—here the doctor lowered his voice
—"he has in his stable a horse-whip,
which will wake you up better than my
ferule."

Philip stood perfectly petrified at this
sudden and most dreadful disclosure. His
knees shook—he dropped his letter—his

teeth chattered; and when the farmer, at a sign from the doctor, approached him with, "Come, my little man, go and get ready; my time is money to me," poor Philip sprawled down on his knees, crying—

"No! no! I don't want to go! Oh, Dr. Gradus, pray let me stay here! I will study! I will; indeed I will! I will sit up all night and construe my Latin, and work out those awful logarithms which nearly crack my head to understand. I'll never say again I can't bear the sight of figures. Oh, I shall go distracted! Oh! oh! oh!"

"No doubt you think you will learn *now*, but by to-morrow you will have forgotten all these fine promises"—and the doctor gave the farmer another sign, who grinned understandingly; then, bringing his great fist down upon the table, and making some glass retorts and all the books bounce, cried in a gruff voice—

"Come, sir, this won't answer; neither I nor my horses can stand here doing nothing. Make your bow to the master, and come along."

Philip struggled, and kicked, and tumbled about, looking as if he was all legs and arms—not a very graceful figure, you may believe; and he cried and screamed, "Let me go-o-o! let me go-o-o!" as the farmer dragged him all the way down stairs, and out of the house. Yes, he screamed louder than ever out of the house, in hopes of attracting some attention from his school-fellows to his sad fate; but not a single boy ran to see who was making such a dismal howling; they were all now in class.

When he was safely stowed away in the wagon, amidst the empty corn-sacks, the servant brought out his trunk of clothes which the doctor had ordered her to pack, and the letter which the now sobbing boy had dropped in the study; then she went back for a moment and returned with some school-books fastened together by a leather strap; and seeing how much Philip appeared to be suffering, she forgot how many times he had thrown her dust-cloth out of the window, and sent her broom and dust-pan flying after it; her heart melted, and she said kindly—

"Never mind, Master Philip; if you doesn't behave, you must expect to be punished; but it'll do you good, like physic. Just you try to be a first-rate boy, and you'll be back here in a good deal less than no time."

"*Master* Philip, indeed!" cried the farmer. "Pretty well for a stable-boy! You'll be plain Phil as long as you live with me, I can tell you. Stop that pla-guy snuffling and sighing, making such a dismal whistling about my ears! it's enough to knock a sloop over. If you are ever so good, you will never make up for the loss of my Jack, and I'll be bound his poor little sister Essie is crying for him 'this very moment."

The wretched boy choked down his sobs, and crept into a corner among the corn-bags, where he hid himself, wiping away the big tears that fell silently. Soon the slow motion of the wagon soothed him. He lay for a while drowsily watching the trees and the wild roses growing on the fences, that sent their faint sweet perfume in to him with a gentle wave of their pretty heads; and presently, as the horses turned into a road which lay through a cool, quiet wood, the myriad leaves of which made a deep shade, our young friend gave a final sigh, and, opening his mouth and shutting his eyes, forgot all his troubles, and snored tunefully to the end of the journey.

After four hours' driving, just as the sun was setting, the farmer turned down a crooked lane, perfectly alive with grass-hoppers, and soon came in sight of a straggling red house, at the door of which stood a nice-looking woman, and a little pale, yellow-haired girl, supported by crutches. In another moment out rushed a very small brown dog, who fairly "barked himself sideways," in his intense joy at seeing his master; then he jumped up so high that he fell over backwards,— the whole time wagging his ridiculous morsel of a tail so fast, that it looked like six tails all going round like a windmill.

The farmer jumped out of the wagon, and, heartily kissing his wife, stooped down and tenderly stroked the soft locks of the little pale crippled child; then lifting her in his arms, he kissed her five or six times, saying between each kiss, in a deep loving voice, "My little Essie—my little Essie."

"My little father," laughed Essie, patting the big man's cheek, "what a dear, good little man you are."

At the sound of her soft, gentle voice,

and the pat of her small hand, the farmer
hugged her closer to his breast.   Then he
looked down into her sweet blue eyes,
and said, "O–h, Essie!"   The great love
that flowed out with these two words, no
pen can show.

"Tell me, little father," whispered Essie, "have you got the bad boy with
you?"

"Yes, big darling," said the farmer.

Then he carried her to the side of the
wagon, and showed her a great, red-faced
boy, fast asleep on the corn-sacks.

"Why, he's asleep!" she said.

"Sound as a top; but we'll wake him
up, my little maid."   So the farmer picked
up a long straw from under the seat, and
drew it across Phil's upper lip.

"Ow! get out," cried the boy, rubbing
his face violently.

Essie laughed, and the farmer tickled
Phil under the nose again.

"Ow! ow!" cried Phil, kicking out

with both his legs, and butting his head against the side of the wagon. "Hang the old fly." Then starting up, he opened his eyes, and stared wildly at Essie and her father.

"Come, Phil," said the farmer kindly, "we're home; get down, and come in the house."

All at once the boy remembered, and with something between an oh! and a groan, he followed his new master.

In they all went—and what a nice little room it was, to be sure! Great bunches of feathery asparagus filled the fireplace; a canary bird, in a pretty cage, hung in the open window, through which the sweet breaths of honeysuckles came floating; not a speck of dust could be found on chairs or table, and the rag carpet was as clean as brooms could make it. Over the mantelpiece was an engraving of Cain and Abel, which Essie did not like; and opposite, one of little Samuel

4

praying, which she did. Through the door facing to that by which they had entered came a sound of frying, and an appetizing fragrance of ham.

Phil flopped sulkily down on the first chair; then he gaped as if the top of his head had got unhinged, and was falling off backwards; then he stretched out his arms till his shoulder-blades cracked, and then he grumbled out—"I am hungry."

"What, already!" exclaimed the farmer. "Why, the girl at Dr. Gradus's said you had eaten one orange, three apples, and a quarter of a pound of lollipops, beside your dinner."

"I don't care! I'm hungry! Oh, what will become of me! Where can my father be gone! Oh! how miserable I am!" whined Phil.

"Poor boy!" said little Essie, her blue eyes filling with compassionate tears; "give me my crutches, please, dear father, and I will go right in the kitchen and hurry the tea."

Her father did as she wished, and oh! then, it would have done you good if you could have seen the little thing hobbling to the kitchen door, and crying out so pleasantly, as she rested on the crutches, to give a smart clap of her hands—"Hurry up, Hannah. Let's have tea before you can say Jack Robinson!"

You would hardly believe how the good woman bustled about after that! She tore to the dresser and got a dish; she flew to the table and caught up a fork; and in a trice the ham was out of the frying-pan, in the dish, and on the table, which was already set in the kitchen; then one, two, three, a dozen hot snowballs of potatoes— that's a funny idea!—were whipped out of a pot in the corner, into a big bowl, and those put on the table, opposite the ham; then the tea was set to steam, and, while that was doing, Hannah skipped

round like a crazy monkey, and thump,
thump, thump, thump, just like that, four
chairs were set to steam—no, I don't mean
that—I mean, to the table; but I'm in
such a hurry to tell it all before you can
say Jack Robinson, you know! and then
tea was ready.

It was all done in two minutes, because
Hannah loved little Essie so dearly; but
she could not help looking rather crossly
at the greedy boy, who hardly waited for
grace to be said, before he began to eat as
if he meant to give himself half-a-dozen
stomach aches, and a horrible nightmare,
when he went to bed, by his gourmand-
izing.

When he could not possibly swallow
another morsel, he pushed back his chair,
and, in five minutes, was in a heavy sleep,
snoring like a trumpet.

"Wife," said the farmer, "if that chap's
father hadn't promised to give our Johnny at least three months of first-rate educa-

tion, if we would consent to this queer experiment, I don't think I *could* keep such a lout about the place."

"How long is he to stay?"

"Why, I tell you, it is to be for three months, if he gives up his lazy, ugly ways; if not, six months; and all this time he's not to know where his parents are; and I've promised to watch him like a cat, so that he don't run away."

"I tell you what, husband," said the good woman, "if any thing will make a good boy of him, it will be living with our little Essie here;" and she looked through the kitchen door, into the sitting, or "living room," as country people call it, at her darling, who was bending her golden curls over a book called "Neighbor Nelly Socks," and laughing out every little while, as if it was very amusing.

All this time Philip was snoring. The farmer's wife let him sleep until Hannah had had her tea, and had washed the plates

and dishes, and made all neat; then she
shook him up and down as if he were a
big bottle of medicine, and, taking his
arm, helped him up-stairs into the garret,
where was a little cot bed in a corner,
with a straw mattress, covered with coarse,
but clean sheets.

"Is — this — my — room?" gasped Philip, with a horror-struck countenance.

"Plenty good enough for a stable-boy,"
answered Mrs. Goodfellow, for of course
you know by this time that she was Johnny Goodfellow's mother.

"But I'm a-f-r-a-i-d."

"Afraid of what?"

"I d-o-n't know.   It's such a big, dark
place."

"Oh, if that's all, there's nothing here
but dried apples and onions; two broken
chairs, which my Johnny has played
horses with many a time, and an empty
poll parrot's cage, which has travelled
with him and his horses, all over the

world, up here in the old garret. Bless your heart! Johnny thinks it's great fun to bring little Essie up here, to play, rainy days. So you say your prayers, and go to sleep; as it is your first night here, I'll leave the light. Good-night."

She left the unhappy boy, who sat on the side of his cot, and stared fearfully around. The little oil lamp gave but a feeble glimmer, and he jumped as if he had seen a ghost, as his eye caught sight of an old great-coat hanging from one of the rafters; then he began slowly to undress. As he took off his jacket a letter fell out of the pocket. It was the one Dr. Gradus had given him from his father, which in his misery he had forgotten. He opened it and read as follows:

"MY DEAR SON—You seem to think that the whole world is made of plum puddings and pie-crust, and that all you have got to do is to eat your way through it, with as little exertion as possible. 'There is no royal road to learning.' If you want to grow up any better than a two-legged donkey, you must study and work.

"If you won't do this, you had better go on all fours at once.

"I shall now make one last effort to rouse you to diligence, and a wish to discover what your brains were made for. At present they are no better than calves' brains, only fit to be boiled and served up with sauce; although you have been told often enough that they were given you for your own use, improvement, and the good of others; that the more you study and cultivate your faculties, the wiser, better, and happier you will be. But this good advice has been thrown away, and I intend to bestow all your advantages upon Johnny Goodfellow, the farmer's son, who loves learning as much as you do pastry and cake; and you are to take his place—groom horses, follow the plough, chop wood, draw water, and do up generally what farmers call 'chores,' which, I believe, means a hundred and fifty different things.

"When you have learned to execute all these things quickly and cheerfully—mind! 1 say *cheerfully*—if you wish to return to your studies, and become something more than a two-legged donkey, I shall be very glad to take you back to your home and my love; but until then, do not expect to hear from your grieving mother, or sorrowful father,

"JAMES WISEMAN."

Here was a terrible letter indeed! and Philip sank down on his bed, and miserably reflected upon his bad habits, and the happy home which now seemed lost forever. Conscience began to be busy with him; and all the little fellows whom he had tormented with his "snapper" appeared tc rise up in the far gloom of the garret, laughing inaudibly, and making faces at him. "Oh," he thought, "if I could only get back to school, I *would* be kind to them, I *would* study, I *would* try to please Dr. Gradus and my parents." In the midst of these very sensible reflections, the trouble of which was, that they came a *little too late*, the light went out, and, covering his head with the bedclothes, Philip lay shaking with foolish fears, till he fell into a troubled sleep. *He forgot to say his prayers.*

The next morning, just after daylight, a sonorous voice resounded through the garret, and seemed to shake the brown rafters— "Phil-ip, Phil, wake up!"

"Yes sir," cried the boy, springing out of bed, and staring wildly. "Why, where am I?"

Alas! it all came back too soon, and Philip felt that he was indeed only a stable-boy, when he saw that a coarse pair of dark blue overalls and rough cowhide shoes had been put on the chair by the side of the bed, in place of his own fine broadcloth pantaloons and patent leather boots. He put the rough clothes on with heavy sighs, not waiting to tie the shoes, as the farmer shouted to him to "make haste and come to the stable."

When he got there, he was taught how to wash and curry the great farm horses, put on halters, and take them to a trough in the farmyard to water. Then he had to bring them back and harness them, and fasten them to the pole of the wagon, for the farmer, who had been loading it with vegetables and fruit to take to market to sell, while Phil was left behind with orders to clean the stables, and prepare the litter for night. He was not alone in these labors, for a man who helped in the fields and garden, worked with him for the present, and gave him a great deal of good-natured advice and assistance.

Phil felt very miserable, almost desperate; but he had the sense to perceive, that the only way to get back to his former station was to do his duty here. So he worked slowly but steadily all day, with many sighs and groans, wiping away a great tear now and then with his shirt-sleeve.

It was certainly lonely dull work; and some of it not very nice; for he had to feed about fifty great pigs, and everybody knows that pigs never use Cologne, and had rather roll in a mud-puddle than take a warm bath with plenty of nicely scented soap. So all the time he was bringing these grunting, snorting, bad-smelling animals their food, which the farm man very properly called "swill," he held his breath till he nearly burst; while the pigs, fighting, kicking, butting, and pushing, ate their dinner in the midst of a regular riot. Oh! I wonder if children ever eat in this fashion?

There was one pleasant duty which

helped to brighten the gloom of the rest. Just before sundown, Essie came to find him, almost skipping on her little crutches.

"Will you come and help me feed the chickens?" she asked, in her sweet song-voice.

Philip ran to her. He did not speak, but she saw that he was glad to come. They both went into the kitchen, and Essie directed him to get a great tin pan, and fill it with rich-looking gold-colored Indian meal. Then she poured hot water into it from a pitcher, while he stirred the meal with a wooden spoon, with all his might and main. Oh, how good it smelt! Phil almost wished he was a chicken.

They went out, and Essie called, "Chick, chick: here, chick, chick." In a moment there was such a scuttling, and clucking, and running! Up they rushed by dozens; and as Phil threw great spoonfuls of the meal, how they did scratch, and snatch, and give each other sudden sly pecks!

It was very funny, Phil thought, and he
and Essie laughed merrily; but only funny, I am sure they would say, for *chickens*.
I do not think any one will ever try to
teach chickens or pigs to eat with knives
and forks, and say, "If you please," and
"Thank you," for what they get; but you
will all agree that neatness and politeness
at the table are expected as a matter of
course from well-bred *children*.

And now the sun had set, like a king
gone to repose, with his crimson and gold
curtains closing round him. In the gorgeous light little Essie stood looking at the
west, the red clouds tinging her pale
cheeks with a faint blush, and shedding
a warm glow over her yellow curling
hair.

"Oh, Phil," she murmured, "how kind
God is to make us such a beautiful world.
Thank you, dear Father in heaven," she
continued, folding her small hands rever-
ently, and looking upwards; then turning

to Philip, "*You* say your prayers. *You* love Jesus, don't you?"

The color rushed into his face, and every nerve in him thrilled, as he looked at the lovely child and heard her words. In a hoarse, broken voice, he answered—

"I haven't said prayers for a long time."

"Oh, Phil, how dreadful! when our Saviour loves you so much, and begs you to bring all your troubles to Him. What made you? Did you forget?"

"I don't know. I suppose so," said Phil, looking down.

She went close up to him, and leaning on her crutches, curled her arms round his neck, and whispered—

"Pray to-night, dear Phil, will you?"

A great sob rose in his throat. With a terribly painful effort, he choked it down, for he was too proud to cry before a girl, and he managed to say, "I'll try," to Essie, whom God seemed to have chosen as

His little minister to lead Phil back to Him.

Just then a lumbering farm wagon came in sight. In it was just the pleasantest-looking old man that ever was seen, with long snow-white hair and blue eyes, still, clear, and bright.

"Well, little bonny bird," he said to Essie, "do you know I have promised to catch you up, and carry you off?"

"Do you mean to lock me up in a fairy palace?" asked Essie, laughing.

"I am to take you to a great big man, who will snap you up, put you in his wagon, and hold you fast, so that you can-not escape."

"Did the big man call me his 'Little Essie?'"

"This is what he said: 'Farmer Hardy, I've got to turn off about two miles from home, on some business. You'll be going past my house; won't you stop and bring my little Essie, on your way home? I will

Little Essie going to meet her father.

be at the cross-roads and meet you, and get my white lamb, and take her back again.' "

"It's *dear* father," said Essie, and she laid down her crutches, and was tenderly lifted into the wagon, and bidding Phil "good-by" for an hour, drove off with good old Farmer Hardy, talking pleasantly with him.

And poor Phil was left behind lamenting; for it seemed as if it grew suddenly dark, as the sound of the wheels got faint and fainter, and at last died quite away. Then he went to the end of the crooked lane, and climbed into the fork of a tree to watch for Essie's return.

You may be sure, when the dear little child was met by her father, and lovingly placed close beside him for the pleasant ride home, she told him how good Phil had been all day, at which Farmer Goodfellow looked very much pleased; and when he and Essie got to where the tree

5

was in which Phil had perched himself,
he was told to jump into the wagon, and
they all came down the crooked lane, just
as the stars were peeping out, three very
happy people.

I don't think you would have known
Phil for the same boy, had you seen how
he flew round, giving the horses their supper, putting them in their comfortable
stalls, and dragging at the wagon, with
the help of the farm man, to get it safely
housed. The boys at the school would
certainly have declared that it could not
be "Philip Badboy," but a sensible, industrious fellow called Philip Wiseman.

And the farmer showed how much he
was gratified, by giving him a seat next
his own at the table, and letting Essie help
him twice to apple-sauce.

"I dare say," said the farmer, "you
will like farming better than Greek and
Latin ; while my son John is all for books.
Learning suits *him* to a T."

Phil blushed deeply, and hung down his head.

"Never mind," said the farmer; "you've got your good points too. To-morrow is Sunday. After you have done your stable-work, you can go to church, and if you listen to our good parson, you can't help improving."

That night Philip knelt down in his lonely garret, and asked God to forgive his many sins, for Jesus' sake. His face was wet with penitent tears when he rose, and God heard his prayer, and saw the tears.

* * * * * * *

Let us go back to the school. You would have thought that Johnny Goodfellow, who was left in place of Philip Badboy, wore a fairy talisman outside of his heart, which made everybody love him, so great a favorite did he become almost immediately. Yes, he wore a charm; but it was *inside* his heart, and

it was called LOVE. Do you know, darling little reader, whom *I* love with all my
heart—that in that sublime chapter in
Corinthians which tells about Charity, it
is *Love* which is meant?   The word in the
original is "Love;" but for good reasons,
and so as not to be misunderstood—because this word "love" has not always a
divine meaning—the translator chose the
word "Charity."   And now, whenever
you read the beautiful chapter, which I
hope you do very often, and, what is
more, *practise its heaven-sent lessons*, always think that "Charity" means the
purest "Love."

How the little fellow did study! It
seemed as if he could not say his lessons
wrong if he tried ; and in play hours, he
frolicked at such a rate with his particular
friend Kriss Luff, who clung to him from
the very first day, that he did not lose his
bright rosy cheeks, as his good mother had
feared.   He wrote her a long letter once a

week, sending many loving messages to his father and darling sister Essie, and not forgetting Phil. And once, when a travelling photographic gallery came up to the school, he had himself taken with his arm round his friend Kriss's neck; and he particularly requested that Kriss should be looking at his watch at the moment, as it would seem such a grand thing, he said, for a boy to have one.

Johnny learned to construe Latin in such a surprisingly short time, that Dr. Gradus forgot one morning to be as pompous as usual, and tapping his new scholar on the back, told him he was an honor to the school, and said he was quite a "multum in parvo," which, I am certain, meant a great compliment, for Johnny colored deeply, while an expression of delight illumined his features. It is a very majestic thing to praise people in Latin; but for my part, I wish Dr. Gradus had talked English, don't you? If you can find out

what "multum in parvo" means, just
write it to me in a dear little letter, directed
to the care of Mr. Sheldon.

Of course Johnny told Kriss all about
his sister Essie; how pretty and good she
was, and how she had to walk with
crutches, because she had hurt her knee
when she was a little bit of a thing, and
the leg that was injured never grew any
more, at which Kriss was dreadfully sorry, and sent his love to her, and a funny
little picture, in an envelope, of a boy who
was pulling out the nose of his sister's
india-rubber doll, and making it at least
half a yard long. And Essie, in return,
sent him a great gingerbread cake, which
she helped to make herself, and Kriss had
what he called "a public dinner" off of
it, and made a fine speech, standing on
top of the pump in the play-ground; after
which he cut a slice of cake for every boy,
all elegantly arranged on cabbage leaves
for plates, upon receiving which they gave

him three ·perfectly tremendous cheers,
and in five minutes more every single
crumb had disappeared.

And Johnny kept rosy and fat, although
he really seemed to live on geography, the
multiplicatior table, and the Latin grammar; but he could play too; for Kriss
declared that he could run faster, jump
higher, swim longer, and shout louder
than any other fellow in the school, which
was·very remarkable, for some of the boys
could run like lamplighters, jump like
kangaroos, swim dog-fashion and crab-
fashion, dive like stones, float like feathers,
stand on their heads under water and bow.
to you with their feet, and as to shouting,
I only wish you could hear them once—
that's all.

*   *   *   *   *   *   *

All the boys agreed that Johnny made
the very best back of them all at leap-frog,
—so strong and square, with his hands
firmly planted on his knees, and looking   ·

between his legs with his round face upside down.　Then he was a capital hand
at mending broken-down drums, toy-carts,
horses, and all manner of playthings.　The
little boys in the school would bring them
to him, and, first hugging him, would coax
him to "make them as good as new," until he declared that the little closet in
his room was a perfect hospital, of which
he was the doctor, and a jack-knife and
Spalding's glue the medicines.

And such wonderful kites as he could
make !　They quite astonished the whole
neighborhood, birds and all.　A famous
one which he made was, as he declared,
a genuine portrait of a round-shouldered,
bullet-headed member of Congress he had
seen, whose brains being made of feathers,
were just the very ones to go off in a high
wind, at a tangent, and never touch any
sensible thing, or cut even a curve in the
air, much less a difficult question.　So the
member of Congress was painted on an

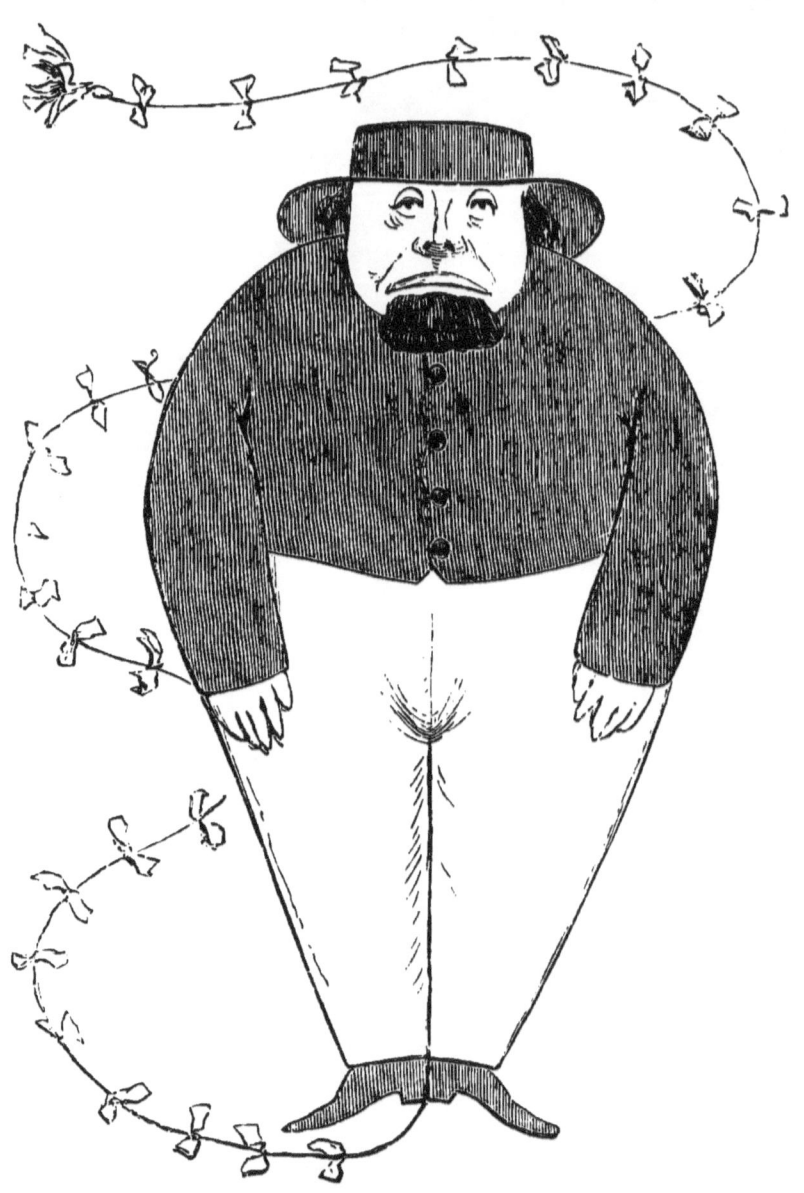

The Hon. Mr. Kite.

immense sheet of tissue paper, and fur
nished with an exceedingly long tail, made
of scraps of cotton-wadding tied on a
string at intervals of four inches, and so
light that it balanced his brains to perfection. When he was finished, he was
dubbed "The Honorable Mr. Kite;" and
many a fine day did the honorable gentleman air his feather-brains over the broad
fields, and look down with his stupid fat
face at the delighted boys, who all took
turns in giving him a "flier."

But perhaps the very best of Johnny's
social accomplishments came out on rainy
days, when he told stories without end, so
excellent was his memory of what he had
read or heard ; and the bright play of his
features added so much to the interest, that
the boys declared, when they came to read
the very same stories in books, as sometimes happened, they did not seem one
quarter as good. I really feel tempted to
tell you one of them, though, like the

boys, you will lose three-quarters of the interest because you do not get it direct from him. Shall I.

Aunt Fanny had read thus far in her manuscript, when she paused, looked up, and repeated, "Shall I?"

"Oh, yes! yes! if you please," cried all the children.

"But it won't seem more than a quarter as entertaining."

"Oh, you funny Aunt Fanny! you know we shall like it just as well—better. But tell us, did *you* hear that jolly Johnny Goodfellow tell a story?"

"Of course I did," she answered, "and this is the way he did it. First, let's all sit down on the carpet."

You would have thought that each of the children had been presented with a fine present, they received this proposition with such delight and so many chuckles. Down they all got in a bunch, with Aunt Fanny in the midst. Then she clasped her hands over her knees, made her mouth into a button-hole, and looked up at a corner of the ceiling, pretending to think. She looked so long, that Fred, full of Johnny Goodfellow and his story, quite forgot he was speaking to Aunt Fanny, and shouted—

"Come, old fellow! we're all waiting; why don't you begin?"

Then suddenly remembering himself, he turned as red as scarlet, and stammered out—

"Oh, I didn't mean——I beg your pardon."

The button-hole mouth broke loose, and Aunt Fanny burst out laughing, as she said—

"That was just what I wanted. Now, attention, squad! Aunt Fanny has jumped over the moon, and Johnny Goodfellow is here in her place to tell you the wonderful tale, a good deal altered, which he read in an English magazine, called

"BROTHER BOB'S BEAR."

ONCE upon a time, a Yankee farmer found he had such a lot of children, that they cost him more than they were worth. So he concluded to emigrate out West, where the old ones could shoot game and plant corn and keep out of mischief, and the young ones could laugh and grow fat by rolling on the prairies and eating hasty-pudding.

He found that he was well enough off, when he got to his new home, to build a very aristocratic log-house. Very few, you know, have more than one room, while his had three—all elegantly ceiled with hemlock-bark, with the smooth side out—quite gorgeous, you may believe.

It was in May that he moved, and the whole summer was before the children to frolic in, and have a grand good time; and the eldest brother, Bob, began the game by shooting a bear who wanted to hug him.   You know a bear's hug is a remarkably tight squeeze, and generally takes your breath away for good.   So Bob declined the honor, and popped a bullet in the bear's cranium, and carried home in his arms a perfect little darling of a cub, for the poor bear was a mother.

Oh, what a welcome the little cub got! It was hugged and kissed all round; and Bob, congratulating himself that it was too young to mourn long for the loss of its mother, solemnly declared that he intended to be a mother to it for the rest of its life. And he kept his word.

The cub, who was named Moses, slept with Bob, always laying his nose in a sentimental manner over Bob's shoulder.   He grew very fast; you could almost see him grow; and there really seemed no end to the bread and milk and mush and butter he would eat.

The first winter he was kind of numb and stupid, and spent a great deal of time in sleeping and sucking his paws. But when the warm weather came on, he was the happiest little bear in the world, following Brother Bob about like a dog, and only miserable when he lost sight of his master. He always woke him in the morning; and as the bear liked to get up early, you see he was quite a blessing to Bob in this respect, as getting up early, according to the proverb, is one of the sure and certain ways of becoming healthy, wealthy, and wise. I always feel the wisdom sprouting out all over me when I get up very early in the morning; but I'm afraid I should spend all the extra money I made by early rising in buying an extra breakfast, for it also makes me so tremendously hungry.

Well, one day Brother Bob had to go a long journey to buy material for building a frame house, of a man who had a sawmill. Moses could not accompany him; and this was a dreadful affliction. Bob had to steal away; and when the bear found he had gone, he commenced a search for him. He went to Bob's bed, and, beginning at the head, poked his nose under the sheets and blankets, and gravely travelled down till he came out at the foot; then he turned and slowly marched up again. He kept this up by the hour, never stopping till he was shut out of the room. He then took possession of all Bob's clothes he could find, and got as far as he could push into the legs of the trousers and arms of the coats, still hoping that his beloved master would be found in some of the dark corners; and Bob's mother, half distracted at seeing the clothes tearing with such rough usage, got them away with great difficulty, and locked them up in a wardrobe.

Then Moses, with tears in his eyes, and grunting with grief, managed to climb to the top of the wardrobe, and seized a large Bible which rested there, and, curling himself up into a round ball, dropped on the floor, hugging the Bible fast. Bob's mother tried to get this away, but the bear showed fight for the first time, and kicked out his hind legs, and gave sly dabs at the broomstick with which she was beating him; but he held the book tight, and Bob's mother had to give up, and come off second best; and what's more, the bear knew it, and made use of his triumph afterward.

When Bob came back, the bear fairly danced for joy, dropping the Bible, and showing his contempt for Bob's mother by taking the butter from the tea-table and eating it before her eyes. His master gave him a good drubbing for stealing, and he submitted to it with perfect indifference, for his dear master might do as he pleased; but when he was not present, butter and honey, and sugar and molasses, were all taken with the utmost coolness; and the poor old lady could not help herself, for he had now grown so large and strong that she was afraid of him.

"Oh, Bob," she said, one day, "your bear is the plague of my life."

"Now, mother," he answered, "you have only got to be resolute, and show that you are not afraid of him."

"But I *am* afraid of him, and he will do me some dreadful harm yet."

"Give him a taste of hot poker, mother, and he'll never bother you again."

"Oh, Bob!" she exclaimed, "I would not do that for the world!"

And so the bear had his own way, and became a very tyrannical member of the family, till something happened which did more than even a mother's remonstrances.

For Brother Bob fell in love. Just at this time the Yankee farmer got a neighbor—a very near one for the West, only

6

five miles off—and this neighbor had a
pretty daughter, seventeen years old; so
what does Bob, who, I forgot to tell you,
was nineteen years old—what does he do
but fall so head over ears in love, that he
declared she was the prettiest and best girl
in the whole universe, which *I* think was
saying a great deal.

But Susan (that was her name) treated
Brother Bob shamefully. She played
tricks upon him; she made fun of him
before his face, and kept him perfectly
miserable; and declared, moreover, that
she did not care half an ear of corn for
him. Here was a pretty state of things!
for even the bear could not comfort the
poor fellow.

But one day Susan and a younger sister
came to take tea with Bob's mother. They
had never seen Moses, and did not know
of his existence. Bob shut the bear up in
his room, in compliment to the guests, and
the afternoon passed off very pleasantly;

that is, to all but Moses, who was highly disgusted at being locked in.

When the time came for Susan and her sister to leave, Bob prepared to see them home through the path in the woods. He ran into his room for his hat, never thinking of Moses, and left the door open, and came quickly out of the house, as Susan, with her teazing ways, had already started.

Down rushed the bear after him, out of the door, up to Bob, seized him in his arms, and hugged him, in his joy, in a way frightful to behold; and Susan, turning, saw Bob in this terrible embrace. She screamed; oh, how she screamed! and instead of running away, *she rushed right up to the bear*, and tried to pull him off, crying and sobbing, "Oh, Bob! dear, dear Bob! you will be killed!" and then fell fainting to the ground.

Ha! ha! Miss Susan, you were found out! But Bob behaved very well; for he caught her in his arms, and said—

"Dear Susan, he is a tame bear; do not be afraid."

The poor girl looked like a broken white lily, trembling at the bear, and ashamed that she had showed Brother Bob how much she cared for him; and when she had recovered her wits, she cried out piteously—

"Oh, I will never come here again !"

"Yes, you will !" said Bob, "now that I know you like me. I'll banish the bear, or put him in prison, or do any thing you wish."

It was wonderful how many faults Bob discovered that the poor bear had after this; and one day when he snatched a pudding from the plate in the very hands of Bob's mother, as she was taking it to the table, he made up his mind that Moses must be chained.

So the bear was fastened to a surveyor's chain, made tight to a stake in the ground. He immediately began walking in a circle round the stake, at the extreme length of the chain, always turning a somerset at one particular point, and only stopping to eat, or look reproachfully at Bob when he came that way. Why he wanted to exercise in this very peculiar fashion, tumbling head over heels at one spot every time he went around, is a good deal more than I know; but I believe all bears who are chained act in this comical way, though it can't be much fun to them.

This was all very well in the daytime, but sure as night came, Moses broke his chain, and did his best to get back into his master's bedroom. Poor fellow! he so wanted to lie at the foot of Bob's bed, hugging an old vest. And at last they had to build a prison for him of logs, with a roof of boards kept on by heavy stones.

The very first night the poor bear was put in this den, he raised the boards off the roof in his desperate struggle to get out and see his beloved master. He got

his head out, and then, oh! ah! alas!
hung by his neck, and was choked to
death—a martyr to his great love for
Brother Bob.

You may be sure, Bob's mother was
rather glad, but, old as he was, Bob could
not help shedding a few tears for his
clumsy, ugly pet. He got a new and
pretty pet before long; and so it came to
pass that the farmer and all his family
soon gave up bewailing the tragical end of
BROTHER BOB'S BEAR.

"There!" said Aunt Fanny; "what do
you think of Johnny's story?"

"Grand!" cried the children. "We
know more about bears now than we ever
did before."

"I wish I could have a bear," said
Peter.

"Come here and I will give you a bear's
hug," cried Fred.

He jumped upon Peter and squeezed

him till both were perfectly red in the
face, and breathed in puffs. Then Fred
kindly offered to give Aunt Fanny a hug;
but she, jumping up and laughing, said
she had no breath to spare. And after a
good deal of skirmishing around, and
making believe to punch each other with
their elbows, dancing and singing—

"There was an old woman,
Who had but one spoon,
And all she wanted
Was elbow room,
Elbow room, elbow room,—
All she wanted
Was ELBOW ROOM"—

they consented to sit down quietly to hear
once more about their friend Philip.

* * * * * * *

At the farm, all this time, Phil had been
improving. Not steadily, for no one becomes good all at once. He would have
his fits of laziness and sulkiness; but the
ministering love and sweet example of

little Essie soon made him ashamed of himself, and try to conquer the enemy, praying to his Father in Heaven for help. You know very well, darling children, that our worst enemies are our evil passions and bad habits, and when we gain a victory over them, all the angels in heaven rejoice, and then God's Holy Spirit descends into our hearts, sending a glow and thrill of happiness all through us.

As Phil grew good-tempered and industrious he began bitterly to regret the advantages he had neglected and lost while at school, and when Johnny's letters were read aloud, his heart would beat violently, and he would say to himself—"Shall I ever be so smart? What a miserable, foolish fellow I have proved myself!"

• One Saturday evening he went softly up to Mr. Goodfellow, and asked—"Won't you please tell me something about my dear father and mother?" and then burst into tears.

"Why, Phil!" cried the farmer, "what's the matter? Your parents are well, and know that you are trying to be a better boy. Don't cry. The time will soon pass; and a little farm learning will not hurt you. If you go on as you have done this two or three weeks past, you'll come out all right, my boy."

The next morning, after his work, Phil washed and dressed himself carefully, and went to church. His history, by this time, was pretty well known, and the good minister, who had become quite interested in him, had not only been to see him, but had always spoken to him kindly when he waited in the churchyard after the service, while the farmer and his wife talked awhile to their neighbors.

On this day, Phil went up to the good clergyman, and, blushing deeply, stammered out, "I should like to speak to you, sir."

"Well, my dear boy," he answered

kindly, "don't be afraid; tell me what I can do for you.

"Oh, sir, if—if—you would only ask Mr. Goodfellow to let me go to evening school. I want to learn—I do indeed."

"Well, that is quite right; but you were at an excellent school. Why did you not study there?"

Phil blushed more deeply than before, but he said, truthfully and manfully, "I neglected my opportunities, sir: I would not learn; and all the boys hated me—because I tormented them; and I did not want to do any thing harder than to walk about with my hands in my pockets—or else to be eating."

"But, my child, did this kind of life make you *happy?*"

"No, sir. I grew tired of every thing, and gaped till I sometimes thought the top of my head would crack off; and I used to wish I could sleep all day as well as all night; but now, oh! how I wish I could

go back and study diligently—although
the farmer and his wife are very kind, and
I could hardly bear to leave dear little
Essie. And I want to see my parents, and
beg them to forgive me"—and here Phil's
lip quivered painfully.

"Well, my son, I will speak to the farmer, and if he consents, you shall come to
me for an hour every week-day evening
and continue your studies."

Phil could hardly believe his ears.

"You, sir! come to you!" he exclaimed, his whole face radiant with joy.
"Oh, thank you, thank you; how can I
ever thank you enough!"

He flew to the good farmer, the minister coming slower, and told him the precious good news, ending with, "Now I
shan't grow up a dunce!"—and I am afraid
I must add that he took one or two great
joyful jumps in the air, at which the minister looked a little grave, as it was Sunday, but did not say one word of reproof,

because he knew that "boys would be boys," and sometimes jumped when they ought to stand as still as a mouse.

It was all settled, and the next evening, just as the stars were peeping out, Phil shouldered his books, which, you will remember, were sent away from the school with him, and almost ran all the way to the parsonage.

It is perfectly astonishing how easy a lesson becomes, if you resolutely drive all other thoughts out of your mind, collect your five wits, and set to work at your book. Phil found it so, to his great delight. The good minister smoothed away some of the difficulties which required a little explanation, and excited his ambition to conquer others; and not being near so pompous as the great Dr. Gradus, though knowing quite as much, he and Phil got on capitally together. He did not learn Greek, Latin, and all manner of hard things, like a flash of lightning, mind you.

If I should be so absurd as to tell you this, you would know I was writing about an impossible boy. But his mind gradually cleared up, because he no longer eat like a glutton, and he slept like a top, and took plenty of healthy exercise, and this has every thing to do with intellect and brain. You know, if you have a terrible headache, or eat a great many buckwheat cakes for breakfast, you can't do your sums. So, if you want to grow up a wise man or woman, try to be a healthy child, full of good-nature, good-temper, activity, and courage. They will greatly increase your ability to learn.

About a mile from Mr. Goodfellow's farm was a beautiful country place, which had lately been offered for sale, and one day, when Phil had been almost three months in his new home, the farmer, as he drew in his chair at the tea-table, said—

"Wife, Woodlawn is bought, and the

owner is coming to take possession next week."

He gave his wife a peculiarly comical look as he said this, and a smile broke over her face, but she did not ask any questions.

Phil did not care who was coming; he was so engaged with his books, and so happy working out in the fields all day, that if he could only have heard from his parents, he would have had nothing left to wish for.

Just at this time, also, there was a public examination at Dr. Gradus's school, where anybody in the company was invited to put the most puzzling questions to the scholars. You may be sure, Johnny was always ready with an answer, except once, when he and the whole school, and all the company, burst out laughing, because a queer old wag of a gentleman, seeing that Johnny was so quick and bright, came out suddenly with this—

"Look here, my fine fellow. Suppose a canal-boat heads east-nor'-west for the horse's tail, and has the wind abeam, with a flaw coming up in the south, and cats'-paws showing themselves, would the captain be justified in taking a reef in the stove-pipe, without first asking the cook?"

I said everybody burst out laughing; but I made a mistake; for Dr. Gradus rose up majestically, and made a speech stuffed full of Latin, in which he observed that "problems like that the gentleman had just given were not to be found in any of *his* books;" at which everybody nearly laughed again—he was so solemn and pompous about a joke. I forgot to mention that Dr. Gradus was an old bachelor, and that accounts for it.

Of course, Johnny's father and mother were present at the examination, with little Essie; and oh! what three proud and happy people they were, when, at the end of it, Dr. Gradus got up to present the prizes, and among the very first names called was Master Johannes Goodfellow. At first they did not quite understand that it was *their* Johnny, because Dr. Gradus turned his Christian name into Latin, which, you know, made it grander; and as Johannes's face,—as he walked up, bowed, and took the splendid book presented to him,—was perfectly radiant with happiness, I don't know but what the Latin had something to do with it. But when he saw his dear father holding out his hand to him, his mother's eyes full of joyful tears, and Essie's rosy lips trembling with excitement and pride in her darling brother, he very nearly burst into tears himself; but controlling his feelings with a strong effort, he grasped his father's hand for a moment, and then went back to his seat.

Kriss, Johnny's particular friend, obtained a prize too; and after they were all distributed, the company were invited to partake of refreshments in the parlors, which consisted of very sour lemonade, and such thin slices of cake, that they were all weak in the back, and fell over double when they were taken up. Of course, nobody ought to be hungry after such a "feast of reason" on Latin grammars, geology, mathematics, chemistry, and I don't know what besides—the very names of which made Dr. Gradus smack his lips with delight. He, no doubt, would have preferred to have dined off of Greek lexicons, with chemical sauce, instead of plumcake, with *comical* sauce (that is, plenty of fun and laughing), which you and I would much rather have, wouldn't we?

Then Johnny introduced Kriss to his sister with great pride and delight; and Essie's sweet smile and soft pleasant voice won his heart, and he immediately told Johnny, in a whisper, that his sister was *such* a dear little girl, and a great deal prettier than he expected, and her lame-

7

. ness ought to make everybody as kind and tender as possible; and moreover, that when he grew up to be a man, he meant to marry Essie, and watch over her, and make her as happy as the day was long.

"Oh, delightful!" cried Johnny; "just fancy! then you'll be my brother. I always wished I had a brother. I don't like the thought of finding that cross Phil at home; it will half spoil my holidays. But we must write to each other, Kriss; and you shall have Essie when you grow up; and then we shall live together all our lives."

So they parted; for after the examination there was to be a month's holidays; and Johnny had as much as he could do to shake hands and bid good-by to the crowd of noisy, merry boys, every one of whom loved him. All the teachers also shook hands, and hoped he would come back; and Dr. Gradus, pushing up his spectacles, and clearing his throat with a tremendous "hem," said that Master Goodfellow quite fulfilled the promise of his name; at which heavy joke everybody nearly died of laughter, and all because it was the great Dr. Gradus who said it.

It was beautiful autumn weather. The leaves were just beginning to turn; the dark green woods were flushing into gorgeous tropical beauty; and four happy people were riding home, their hearts full of gratitude and peace, beyond all price.

But when they drove into the crooked lane, didn't the little brown dog bark himself more sideways than ever before, in his frantic joy at hearing Johnny's voice, for it was now quite dark; and didn't Hannah, and the farm man, and Phil, rush out and cry, "Hurra! here they are!"—and Phil's voice sounded so hearty and pleasant, that Johnny shook hands with him immediately, and said, "How are you, old fellow?" as if they had been friends a

year, which made Phil very happy, for he
had been quaking at heart lest Johnny
should not speak to him at all, knowing
what a bad boy he had been.

As they were sitting at the tea-table,
Phil said—

"There is a note for you, sir, on the
table in the living-room."

"Oh, is there? Hannah, will you bring
it here? It looks like something important," he continued, as he took it in his
hand. "Hm—hm—hm. Well, wife, what
do you think it is? An invitation for all
of us to spend to-morrow evening at
Woodlawn."

"Indeed!" said Mrs. Goodfellow, with
a bright but peculiar smile on her face.
"Phil is invited, of course?"

"Certainly; and I am glad and proud
to say that I know he will do himself
credit now, wherever he goes. Our good
minister is to be there too."

"Oh, I am glad of that!" said Phil;

"he is my best earthly friend—" He stopped, and his eyes filled with tears.

"What is the name of the family who have bought Woodlawn?" asked Johnny.

"Such a curious chap as it is!" answered the farmer, laughing. "Never mind the name till to-morrow."

That night there was another cot-bed put in the garret, and Phil and Johnny had a long affectionate talk together. Phil frankly told all about himself, and what Essie and the good minister, with God's blessing, had helped him to do; and Johnny cheered and encouraged him, and told him that he had no doubt but that Phil's parents had heard of his good conduct, and might be expected at the farm almost any day.

But the poor little fellow suffered terribly himself while he was saying all these kind things, for, as you know, Phil's gain would be his loss. If Mr. Wiseman was convinced of his son's reformation, Johnny must go back to farm work, and resign his precious hopes of growing up a learned man. His kind father had not yet paid all the money for his farm; he could not afford to hire another boy in his dear son's place; and now a few months in winter at the district school was all that Johnny must expect.

But he got up the next day bright and happy. It was something—yes, indeed, it was a great deal—to have such a home as his; and after he had washed, dressed, and said his humble, thankful prayers, he was quite ready to race eagerly out with Phil and the little brown dog, and see which could get to the end of the crooked lane. and back again first.

It was lucky that the little brown dog's tail was fast at one end, and the hair on it not a wig, for he certainly would have shook it off, and every single hair out, if incessant and furious wagging would have done it; and the boys and the dog seemed to have each taken a dose of laughing-gas, they flew hither and thither in such a ridiculous way, just because they were so happy.

Then Johnny helped Phil with the horses and the rest of the farm work, and the little brown dog helped too by getting between their legs and nearly upsetting them half a dozen times, and by riding on one of the horse's backs to water, barking the whole time to make him hurry, which, of course, was very funny, and made the boys laugh heartily.

And when they went in to breakfast, there was Essie, with a welcome shining in her sweet blue eyes, and her Bible all ready to read a chapter, before her father asked a blessing on the labors and pleasures of the day.

The day was soon spent in cheerful work, and in the evening they all prepared for their visit to Woodlawn. Phil made himself as neat as possible in his farmer's-boy Sunday suit. He thought first of asking Mr. Goodfellow to let him wear the fine broadcloth clothes in which he came to the farm, but he said to himself a moment afterwards—

"No; I am only a farm-boy now; I will make no pretence to be any better, until my father gives me leave."

He did not need the fine clothes to improve his appearance, for his excellent habits had made such a change, that he would hardly have been known for the same boy. His eyes were bright, his manner animated, and he had learned to be unselfish, industrious, polite, and kind to all—though not without many hard struggles and constant prayer.

As the party drove into the great gate of Woodlawn, and up the long beautiful avenue, they heard the sound of music, and a hundred colored lanterns met their eyes suspended from the trees. They had the effect of enchantment; and Essie said she was sure she saw little fairies dancing in the shaded alleys on either side, and peeping and smiling at her from the bushes. The boys laughed, but they too felt the strange magic of the scene ; and when they arrived at the brilliantly lighted entrance, they were prepared, they thought, for all manner of wonderful events.

After taking off bonnets, shawls, and hats, they were ushered into a small room, the walls of which were covered with beautiful paintings, at which both the boys gazed with delight. Two immense closed doors, opposite the windows, led into another room, from which sounds of laughing and talking proceeded.

Presently the good minister came into the small room, and it was delightful to witness the mixture of respect and grateful affection with which Phil hastened to meet him, and place a comfortable arm-chair for his use.

"Our host and hostess will be here very

soon," he said. "Meanwhile, Philip, if you like, I will ask you and my friend Johnny some questions about your studies."

The boys were delighted, and immediately placed themselves before him, their arms around each other's necks.

Question after question was poured out, and readily answered by the boys in turn —Johnny sometimes having to prompt Phil, and Phil quite as often helping his friend; while the farmer, his wife, and Essie listened with delighted attention: *and two others listened*—for a door behind the boys had been softly opened, and a gentleman and lady stood with the rest, their faces beaming and radiant with love and eagerness.

The good minister saw them, and turning to Phil, he said—

"My dear boy, you have done so well, not only in your studies, but in what is of far more importance, in conquering your bad habits, that all that there is left to wish for is, that your parents might take you back to their home and hearts."

The lady gave a sudden start towards him at this, but the gentleman laid his hand gently on her arm.

"Oh, sir," answered Phil, his lip quivering, "will they ever love me again? Can they ever forgive me?"

"Oh, yes! yes! my own darling boy!" screamed the lady.

Philip turned quickly around, became deadly pale, staggered towards her, and fell nearly fainting into the outstretched arms of his mother; while his father, seizing his hand, cried—

"God bless you, my son! God bless you! You have done nobly. You have made us very, very happy."

Then the rest went softly out of the room, and Phil had a few moments of blissful joy. He curled his arm around his mother's neck, and kissed her over and

over again. He hugged his father with
eager affection ; and then darted back to
his mother—laughing, crying, now smooth-
ing her hair, now crumpling her beautiful
lace collar—perfectly beside himself with
ecstasy.

All at once a band of musicians struck
up a martial air, the great sliding-doors
moved back, and Phil's father and mother,
taking his hands, went forward and introduced him to the company, for they were
the owners of Woodlawn. All knew his
story—for you can't keep such a thing
secret in a country place—and they looked
at him with such intense interest, that he
was becoming confused, when who should
dart forward to welcome him but Kriss
Luff and half a dozen of his old school-
mates, all wanting to shake hands at once,
and this making him laugh, he was soon at
his ease.

Oh, what a delightful evening it was !
They played games and sang, they laughed

and frolicked—the good minister joining in every thing, like a real Christian as he was. They partook in moderation of all manner of nice things which were loading down a table in the dining-room, and each one went home with the recollection of a delightful evening well spent.

Of course, Phil stayed at Woodlawn, and that was one little drop of unhappiness to the kind people with whom he had lived so long, and who had learned to love him very much. They could not bear to part with him. But Johnny was made so happy, that I do not think he knows to this day whether he walked home on his head or like other people; for Mr. Wiseman, patting his sturdy shoulders, said to him—

"Well, my son, are you tired of school yet?"

"Oh dear, no, sir. I love my books. I even love Dr. Gradus."

"Well, that last *is* convincing; so if

your good father, to whom I owe more than I shall ever be able to repay, will permit me to find him a farm-boy, you shall go to school and through college with Phil, and, if you like, choose a profession afterwards, still under my care."

"Hurra! hurra!" cried Kriss and all the boys; "Johnny Goodfellow is coming back to school. Philip *Badboy* has flown to the moon, and Philip WISEMAN is to come in his place. It's the jolliest thing that ever happened. Three cheers for Mr. Wiseman."

They gave three cheers and a "tiger," a big one too, little Essie helping.

"Now," said Kriss, who had voted himself master of ceremonies, "three cheers for Farmer Goodfellow."

They were given, Phil hurraing with such a will, that he got perfectly crimson in the face.

"Now, three cheers for little Essie," said Kriss.

If Phil *could* have made more noise, he would have done so this time; as it was, in his eager desire to honor Essie, he hurraed himself sideways, like the little brown dog, and nearly cracked his throat.

"*Now*, boys, three cheers for Phil, our *new* friend."

Didn't they give it, though! YES, THEY DID, and such a royal Bengal tiger to end with, that the very windows rattled again.

To the children who do not live in New York, I ought to say that we have a splendid regiment of soldiers, called the "Light Guard," who, whenever they cheer, always say, "Hurra! hurra! hurra! ti-g-a-r!" I don't know why they do it, but this is what is meant by "three cheers and a tiger."

Phil bade the farmer, his wife, and little Essie good-night with tears in his eyes, promising to come and see them every day. Mr. Wiseman had invited Kriss and the other boys to stay a week at Woodlawn, which was a most delightful fact to know and experience. A merry, merry week they all had, and you may be sure Johnny was included in every day's pleasure, and Essie was with them very often.

And now, my darlings reading this, do you think it likely that Mr. Wiseman will ever have to send Philip away again? I do not, and I hope you are of the same opinion; but if you would like me to keep one eye on his future movements, and write to you about them, just let me know, won't you?

*   *   *   *   *   *   *

"That's all," said Aunt Fanny. "What do you think of it, my merry men and ladies? Will Philip Badboy Wiseman do for a beginning?"

"It's perfectly splendid!" cried the children.

"And you don't mean to eat greedily of flower-pot pudding after this, or snap each other's legs with knots in your pocket-handkerchiefs ?"

"Oh no, dear Aunt Fanny. This pop-gun has made us better already. We mean to be ever so kind, industrious, and unselfish after this."

"I wish I had a kite like Johnny's," said Peter.

"Who knows, if you try to be a loving, obedient child, but what the Honorable Mr. Kite may call upon you next spring, all ready for an airing. I'll have a talk with my friend Johnny about it."

"Oh goody! will you?" cried Peter, jumping straight up and down in the air. "My! how good I'll be! I'm going to begin right away ;" and he sat down, solemn and stiff, twirling his thumbs one over the other, and saying, "Look at me! Only see how good I am!" while the rest laughed merrily at the joke.

Then Aunt Fanny had a kind kiss from all, and bade them good-night.

8

The next time Aunt Fanny came she had a funny and rather mischievous twinkle in her eyes. She did not say a word, while she unfolded her manuscript but quietly read out the Pop-gun printed above, and then said her story was called by the comical title of

THE DOG'S DINNER-PARTY.

THE children looked at each other, wondering what was coming, then fastened their eager eyes on the reader, who began as follows :

Once upon a time there lived a funny, bustling, little old gentleman, who thought that dogs, horses, cats, and monkeys, ought to live just as he did ; that is, first and foremost, to behave with perfect politeness, learn to read and write, sit at the table and eat their meals with knives and forks, and sleep in French bedsteads, all tucked up warm. He even insisted on their wearing clothes and patent leather boots, and they ran clattering about the house on their hind legs, with trousers and coats on, and their tails dangling out behind, like a pocket handkerchief out of a pocket.

The little bustling old gentleman was a

bachelor. He had tried about twenty-nine
times to get married, but the ladies, one
and all, insisted that the dogs, cats, and
monkeys must be turned out of the house,
if they consented to come in, which was
very disagreeable and unreasonable, and
made the old gentleman so mad, he said to
himself he would see them to Jericho first;
so making each one in turn a very low
bow, for he was the very pink of politeness, he took himself off, and that was the
last of getting married.

So his family consisted of four fine dogs,
six beautiful cats, eight comical monkeys,
one fat cook, and one fat coachman, two
thin housemaids, and nobody knows how
many grooms and footmen—and they all
lived together, a great deal happier than
Barnum's happy family, and what do you
suppose was the reason? Why, they were
taught by the bustling little old gentleman
to be *perfectly polite.* I forgot to tell you
that his name was Lord Chesterfield.

One day Beppo—one of the family—a handsome brown and white spaniel, went out for a walk. As soon as he got out of sight of the house, he dived into a bramble bush, and scratched off all his clothes, for they plagued him to death, and he trotted joyously along, whistling—

" With reading, and writing, and riches,
 For once in my life, I have done!
I've got rid of that old pair of breeches;
 So, hurrah! my brave boys, for some fun!"

Presently he came to a fine river, and was just thinking he would take a swim, when he heard a piercing scream, and something went splash into the water.

Beppo rushed to the brink just in time to see a little golden-haired child disappear under the rippling waves.

In he dashed, like a flying-fish, swam like lightning to the spot, and caught the little child's dress in his mouth; then turning, swam back, and laid it, drenched and gasping, on the green bank, just as the nurse, her face white with terror, and her limbs trembling, was struggling to reach the shore.

The poor woman caught the beautiful child in her arms and kissed her, and thanked Heaven for her rescue. Then she patted and hugged Beppo, who stood wagging his tail and shaking the water out of his long silky hair. "Ah, madam," he said, with a very polite bow, and his fore-paw on his heart, "I am truly grateful that I was made a spaniel: if I had been a stupid poodle-dog I should have been afraid of the water, and the poor little darling would have been drowned."

"Why!" exclaimed the nurse in astonishment, "is it possible you can talk?"

"Yes, ma'am, my master, the Lord Chesterfield, will have it, though I'd much rather bark; and he makes us eat at the table out of plates, and cut our food with knives and forks, when I think a marrow-bone to gnaw, out in the court-yard, is as nice again ; but he says gnawing bones is perfectly dreadful, and we must learn to eat politely."

" Well, that is very funny ! I shall tell about it as soon as I get home."

So the nurse hastened away, with the pretty child, and was soon telling the frightened mother how little Lucy had run away from her, and tumbled into the river, and how the beautiful spaniel, who could talk like a Christian, had saved her life.

The grateful mother went out the next morning and bought a splendid gold collar, and had this inscription engraved upon it : " *For the noble and brave dog Beppo, who saved little Lucy's life.*"

When the parcel came, the little bustling old gentleman opened it, and reading the words on the gold collar, called Beppo to him.

" Why, only look at this splendid collar, my good fellow," he cried ; " why did you not tell me of your adventure ?"

"I only did my duty," Beppo modestly answered.

"Ah! I am quite proud of you. I shall give you a dinner-party, and you shall carry round the invitations yourself."

"May I invite little golden-haired Lucy?" asked Beppo. "I should like to *so* much."

"Certainly," said Lord Chesterfield; "suppose you write the note yourself; it will be a very delicate attention."

Down sat Beppo, joyously, and soon he had penned this fine invitation:

"Master Beppo wishes you to dine with me to-morrow at five o'clock.

"Miss Lucy Hill."

This was not exactly the right way to word it, but you see his education was not yet completed.

Then the little bustling old gentleman wrote the rest of the notes; for Beppo was rather slow, and ran his tongue out in the most fearful manner, in his anxiety to spell the words right, and then they were nicely sealed up in envelopes, and he put them all together in a pretty little basket.

And now the coachman was ordered to bring out the state carriage and four horses, and Beppo, sitting up inside on his hind-legs, very grand, and no doubt exceedingly uncomfortable, carried the notes of invitation to the most fashionable dogs of his acquaintance.

Three of the dogs to be invited lived in the house, as you know; but they had notes as well as the rest, for that is the way to be perfectly polite. I dare say you have many a time heard people say something like this—

"Oh, it don't make any difference what there is for dinner when *you* come, because we are so intimate; but I should be mortified to death, not to have every thing nice when General Fusbos is invited, as he is such a stranger."

This is abominable manners—as if you ought not to treat those you love far better than a stranger. It always makes me very indignant when such a remark is made to *me;* and I sincerely hope you will profit all your life by this hint about *true* politeness from our friend Beppo.

You can't have a great many at a dinner party, you know; so you must be careful to invite the most agreeable people, and as many ladies as gentlemen. Beppo knew this as well as you, and so you may be sure he had taken great pains to have a pleasant party.

The next morning there were a great many people ringing at the little bustling old gentleman's door, and each one left a note.

Beppo ran into a corner with them, as fast as they arrived, and read them in a great hurry. At last one came, very pretty, of a three-cornered shape, and smelling of roses. The moment Beppo

opened it, and glanced at the contents, he
danced around the room for joy, waving
the note in the air with one of his fore-
paws. Then he rushed up to his master,
exclaiming—

"She's coming! my Lord Chesterfield,
she's coming! Just fancy how delightful
to have her sweet face and golden curls
among our hairy muzzles! Oh, we must
be very polite, and make her as happy as
possible."

It was a lovely summer's day. The sun
turned the ripples of the river into shifting
gold, and there was singing, and buzzing,
and whispering, and laughing everywhere;
all felt kind and loving. Even the hide-
ous old scarecrow in the cornfield allowed
Beppo, in his joy, to dash at him and play-
fully throw him down, bang! on his old
red nose, and he never once attempted to
get up; for he said, in his pine-wood
heart—

"I'm a brute, after all, to frighten the

poor birds out of their wits. I'll just lie down here and take a nap, and let the dear little things have a good time for once."

Oh, it was charming to see that even an old scarecrow could be polite, which, after all, is only another name for loving-kindness.

Just before five o'clock, the nurse brought little Lucy, dressed in blue, and looking like a fairy. Strange to say, although only four years old, she was not in the least frightened, but put her soft white arms around Beppo's neck, and said, "Oh, I love oo, good dog!" and hugged him so kindly, that he would have given all the world to have had her tumble into the water again, so that he might save her life once more.

The little bustling old gentleman took her by the hand, and showed her all over his curious old house, with its suits of rusty armor, great stag horns nailed to the walls, and queer black-looking paintings;

and Beppo followed wherever they went, gently wagging his tail, and answering every question with admirable politeness.

And now all the dogs who had been invited had come, and were sitting in the parlor waiting for the dinner-bell to ring, talking and laughing as pleasantly and properly as the king, or the president, or you, or I.

Of course, the first thing any one said, after "How-de-do?" was, "It's a fine day!" because that's the solemn rule in all polite society. Then, of course, they went on to say it was worse weather last week, and would be better weather next week; and after about a dozen more deeply interesting remarks upon the weather, the dinner-bell rang, and made them all jump. But the very next instant they sat down again, trying to look as if they were in no sort of hurry, as it would have been very bad manners to rush pell-mell down stairs. Everybody knows that.

First the little bustling Lord Chesterfield stepped out, leading Lucy with the utmost consideration and politeness. Then Beppo made a low bow to a very respectable old lady-mastiff, and begged the honor of handing her into dinner, to which she graciously consented. Then a very tall staghound, with an uncommonly sharp nose, paired off with Flora, a beautiful pointer; while a large, grave, middle-aged Newfoundland dog made himself agreeable to an Italian greyhound of no particular age; at least she never liked to tell how old she was, and almost always had the snuffles. Then a pert little black-and-tan terrier skipped up to a coquettish King Charles, and said "would she make him the happiest dog in the world?" upon which she shook her silky ears, and putting her head on one side, and half shutting her beautiful black eyes, lisped out "she would;" while a fat poodle, invited because she was so exceedingly genteel, and a Skye terrier, also used to the very best society, brought up the rear; and thus they marched two and two, with the utmost propriety, into the dining-room.

And now see this elegant party at the table. The little bustling old gentleman at the foot, and Beppo, whose back is turned to you, at the head, with Lucy at his right hand.

I forgot to tell you that our friend had requested a private interview with my Lord Chesterfield, about an hour before dinner.

"Well, sir, what do you wish?" he asked.

"My dear master," said Beppo, respectfully, "you know very well that the dogs who will come to my dinner-party will none of them have on coats or pantaloons, or hooped skirts. I do not wish to mortify them, so please let me wear my natural suit for this once, and only my gold collar."

The little bustling old gentleman turned

upon him with a look of rage, enough to petrify a milestone.

"Is this your gratitude?" he roared, "when I am spending all my days in teaching you to live and dress like a gentleman?"

Then, recollecting all of a sudden that he was setting a very bad example of politeness, he put on a remarkably sweet expression, and added in the mildest tone—

"Excuse me; I forgot myself. I believe —well—yes, upon the whole, as this party is given in your honor, you may do as you please to-day."

"Bow, wow, wow!" barked Beppo, in a perfect ecstasy of delight, and leaping with all four feet in the air. "Bow, w-o-w-w! Oh, my goodness!" he continued, suddenly stopping; "I forgot *myself*, or rather *you*, sir. Please to forgive me; I could not keep the bark in; and it is utterly impossible to stop wagging my tail, I am so happy."

"Ah! how short is life!" sighed Lord Chesterfield; "I am afraid I shall die before my dogs, cats, and monkeys come to perfection!"

But you ought to have seen how elegantly they arranged themselves at the table, bowing and smiling the whole blessed time. It was something worth looking at, I can tell you—all sitting up as fine as you please, five on each side. The waiters, who were rigged out in regimentals, tied white napkins around their necks, at which, I must confess, there was some snarling and a bark or so, and one or two tried to wriggle out of them; but at a grave, severe look from my Lord Chesterfield, they gave up with a low whine, which was much better than could have been expected.

Beppo had a fine piece of beef to carve, and his master a pair of roasted chickens; but all the rest of the dishes were pies of different kinds of birds—pigeon-pie, snipe·

9

pie, woodcock-pie, poll-parrot-pie, owl-pie, cat-bird-pie, and booby-pie, for a booby is a bird as well as a dunce.

Oh, my goodness! how they *did* want to dive into these delicious pies with their paws. If they had dared, they would have behaved exactly as most people do on board of steamboats, where they pounce on all the dishes they can reach at once, and empty them pell-mell on their plates. I have seen oysters, pie, roast beef, salt fish, and ice cream, all mixed up on the same plate—a perfectly horrible mess; and that was because these greedy people had not the first idea of politeness or courtesy one to another, and the want of it made them behave like pigs.

"Shall I help you to a slice of the chicken, madam?" said Lord Chesterfield to Lucy.

"If you please," said Lucy, with a pretty little bow and smile.

"What part do you prefer, madam?'

"I like the merry *sort*, if you please,"
answered the dear little thing—meaning
the merry *thought*.

Now this was perfect good manners.
Some people would have said, "Any part
—I'm not at all particular," and would
have been very impolite, for then the
carver would not be sure he should suit
them ; so, when you are asked, always
choose a part.

"Will *you* have chicken ?" asked Lord
Chesterfield of the respectable old lady-
mastiff.

"Oh, oh ! give it to *me*! *I* want some,"
squeaked out the little black-and-tan terrier, quick as a flash, before the old mastiff
could utter a syllable.

What an awful look he got from the
bustling little old gentleman ! and the mastiff faced round upon him with, "Sir,
you're a disrespectful puppy," and glared
in a way to frighten him into fits ; while
the stag-hound opposite stuck his sharp

nose up in the air, and remarked in a
whisper to Flora, the beautiful pointer,
that "really, young America was getting
too impudent for any thing."

Beppo looked imploringly at his master
to forgive little Snap this time, as he was
young and silly, and hastened to put a delicious cat-bird, with crust and gravy, on
his plate; and after this the dinner went on
splendidly, except that the greyhound of
no particular age kept her tongue waggling
out of her mouth very nearly the whole
time, on account of the snuffles, which pre-
vented her from breathing freely. It was
not very elegant conduct, but as she
couldn't help it, nobody looked at her;
and that, you'll own, was the politest
way of behaving under the circumstances.
The fat poodle and the Skye terrier talked
a little in French about it, to be sure,
but as nobody else understood what they
said, and as they smiled all the time, the
rest took it for granted that they were

admiring their neighbors, and felt highly gratified.

Everybody ate and drank with all the decorum and delicacy of our city aldermen, who ought to be held up as examples of courtesy, honesty, and moderation, to the whole universe. They did not leave so much as a bone on their plates; but I am sorry to say they were in rather too much of a hurry at dessert, for most of them burned their mouths severely with the hot cracker pudding, and Snap, the black-and-tan terrier, declared that it must have been made of fire-crackers.

But, take it all in all, it was a splendid entertainment; and, after it was over, the ladies went back to the parlors, and talked about the last fashions. "Ears were to be cut off closer than ever, for terriers," said the King Charles; and "red, white and blue collars were considered rather old-timed," was observed by the beautiful pointer; "that is, unless the army did something decided *at once*, then they would be the rage again immediately." The gentlemen of course talked of nothing but money, *money*, MONEY, as men, the dogs!? always do, when they get together, and if Lord Chesterfield had not made the signal to move, they would have stayed there talking about money to this day.

Lucy had taken the pretty little King Charles spaniel in her lap, and they had a most delightful chat together, which ended in their vowing everlasting friendship to each other, and promising to exchange visits every day, for, as the King Charles was one of Lord Chesterfield's family, this could be very easily done.

When the gentlemen came up stairs, they had coffee, and then, as it was getting dark, the little bustling old gentleman ordered the gas to be lighted, and proposed some music. First, Lucy played " Old Dog Tray," with one little white finger on the piano, and then she lisped out, in her sweet way, " I know a pretty 'tory."

"Ah! tell it!" cried all the company, gathering gently round her, for there was no pushing, or squealing—"Here, let *me* come in! don't crowd so!" No, indeed! for that would have been any thing but polite. They all fastened their eyes on the lovely little girl, who stood resting her arm on Beppo's neck, so proud and happy to have it there, and in her sweet voice, like a robin's song, she began:

> " A—doo was faller fas,*
>> A—'tar bedan a—bink,
> I heard a voice, a—said,
>> " *Dint*, pitty teeter, *dint!*"
> A—looker in a—hed,
>> A—'fore me I a—pied
> A snow 'ite mount a—lamb,
>> 'Ith a maiden at a—side.
> " No ozzer seep—a—near;
>> A—lamb was a—ll aloney,
> And by a 'ittle cord
>> Was fasser to a toney,
> Ith—ith—

* The dew was falling fast, the stars began to blink, I heard a voice—it said 'Drink, pretty creature, drink!' &c."— *Wordsworth's poem of the "Pet Lamb."*

"Oh! I tant say any more," said Lucy. "What a pity!" and she bent down her lovely golden head, and blushed.

"Oh yes, what a pity!" echoed all the company. "It was so sweet; but we thank you very much for this; it was beautiful!"

"Will oo sing for me?" asked Lucy.

"Certainly," they all cried with the utmost readiness; "our voices are not very good, and will sound horridly after your sweet tones, but you may be sure we shall do our best."

They selected a hunting song with a chorus, and sure enough, with the exception of the stag-hound, whose voice was melody itself, you might have supposed it a compound of distressed rats, an old pump-handle, ungreased cart-wheels, a poker on a tin pan, and the spiritual rappers quarrelling together; for it was all squeal, howl, whine, grunt, and groan, of the most dismal description; but as they really tried with all their might and main to sing a good song, everybody looked pleased, because they took the will for the deed, and made the best of it. Do you observe that, my young friends? · Well, never curl your lips with contempt, or make fun of any honest, kind-hearted effort to entertain you. Try to be pleased and thankful: *take the will for the deed*, and, my word for it, you will find a delicious glow come into your heart, and a lovely expression in your eyes; all your ugly thoughts will fly away to the bottomless pit, and you will find yourself really loving the one you meant to ridicule.

Presently there came one of those long, solemn pauses which *will* take place, do your best, when you have company, and Lord Chesterfield hastened to propose a game. As they were nearly all young and frisky, *with the truest politeness*, he proposed a frolicsome play, though he would much rather have had a sober talk on politics himself. Mind this, if you have a little party, don't insist on doing what *you* like best, and taking all the prettiest and best things, but study the wishes of your guests, and do what pleases *them* most.

So Lord Chesterfield proposed the game of the " Family Coach," to assist their digestion, which was hailed with bounds of delight by all except the old lady-mastiff, and the middle-aged Newfoundland dog, who preferred to take a quiet chat together, which ended in a nap on the sofa; but as they smiled and nodded to each other all the same, the rest concluded they were only shutting their eyes, as very sentimental people do when they talk, and so no offence was taken at their sleeping before company, and the poor old things had a very refreshing time of it.

The little bustling old gentleman appointed himself master of ceremonies, and there not being dogs enough for a grand frolic, introduced a few of the cats and monkeys; who were so enchanted at the chance to come in, that they frisked, and danced, and made a very narrow escape of screaming for joy and becoming perfectly riotous with the fun of the thing ; and that, you know, would not have been polite.

I have a great mind to write down the way Lord Chesterfield made them play this game. I think you will like to know. So here it is.

Usually, you must invent a story about the "Family Coach," as you play ; but unless you are very bright and quick about it, there is not much fun. The next time you have a little party, play this game as it is set down here. I have never seen any written before, and I think, if you use this story, you will have a real funny time.

In the first place, Lord Chesterfield gave them all a part or name, which they must by no means forget, and the point is, that when your name is called, you must get up instantly, twirl around quickly, and sit down again; and when "Family Coach" is mentioned, *everybody* in the play must get up instantly, twirl around quickly, and sit down again.

There were little Lucy and twenty-eight dogs, cats, and monkeys to play, and they each took one of these parts:

1. Off-leader ⎤
2. Near-leader ⎟ Horses.
3. Off-wheeler ⎟
4. Near-wheeler ⎦
5. Reins.
6. Traces.
7. Pole.
8. Whip.
9. Box.
10. Fore-axles.
11. Hind-axles.
12. Fore-wheels.
13. Hind-wheels.
14. Dog's tail.
15. Lamps.
16. Foot-board.
17. Steps.
18. Windows.
19. Doors.
20. Linch-pin.
21. Hubs.
22. Spokes.
23. Springs.
24. Coachman.
25. Footman.
26. Old lady.
27. Fat poodle.
28. Coach-dog.
29. Blinders.

Then the good old gentleman began, speaking rather quickly—

"Once upon a time, in a certain tumble-down old house in the country, there existed a family heir-loom, in the shape of a FAMILY COACH."

All the dogs, cats, and monkeys bounced up with such a whirl, that they looked like whipping-tops, with their own quickly whisking tails for whips, and dear little Lucy, in her haste and delight, tumbled over sideways, and fell softly on the carpet. She did not hurt herself the least bit, but jumped up laughing, to Beppo's great joy, and the play went on.

"To be sure, the FAMILY COACH was rather worn out: the *wheels* were none of the best; the *axles* were nearly rotten; the *linch-pins* were rusty; the *box* tottering, and the whole FAMILY COACH decaying.

"But then the *old lady* who owned it thought it worth all the new ones from

here to Kamtschatka.   The *fat poodle* and
the *coach-dog* couldn't live without it.
The *fat poodle* barked, and the *coach-dog*
wagged his *tail* for joy whenever it appeared.   Indeed nobody knew whether
the *old lady*, the *fat poodle*, the *coach-dog*,
the *coach-dog's tail*, the *coachman*, or the
footman, was most delighted at the event,
when one day the *old lady* ordered out the
FAMILY COACH.

"Immediately the *footman* told the
coachman, the *coachman* told the *coach-
dog*, the *fat poodle* heard of it and barked,
and the FAMILY COACH groaned in every
part under the rubbing and the scrubbing
that was bestowed upon the *pole*, the *reins*,
the *traces*, the *box*, the *fore-axles*, the *hind-
axles*, the *fore-wheels*, the *hind-wheels*, the
lamps, the *foot-board*, the *steps*, the *windows*, the *doors*, the *linch-pins*, the *hubs*,
the *spokes*, and the *springs*.

"At last, the *off-leader* and *near-leader*
the *off-wheeler* and *near-wheeler*, were har-

nessed to the *pole* and *traces;* the *blinders*
and *reins* were in apple-pie order; the
lamps were lit, and the *coachman* mounted
the *box;* the *footman,* the *foot board;* the
old lady got inside, and the *fat poodle* was
following, when, lo and behold! the *coach-
dog* got jealous, seized the *fat poodle* by
the leg, and made him bawl, 'Ki-i! ki-i!'

"Then the *coachman* flourished his
whip, the *footman* fell off the *foot-board*
laughing, and the *old lady* nearly fainted.
But a crack of the *whip* on the *coach-
dog's tail* made him let go, and the poor
fat poodle got inside with a piece out of
his leg; the *leaders* and *wheelers* pranced
and danced, the *axles* groaned, and the
FAMILY COACH started.

"For some time all went on beautifully;
the *wheels* rolled smoothly around; the
leaders and *wheelers* trotted comfortably
along; the *coachman* only cracked his
whip for show; the *footman* amused himself by going to sleep; the *old lady* nod-

ded inside; and the *fat poodle* stared out of the *windows* and *doors*, and grinned and made faces at the *coach-dog*, who had to run underneath.

"Presently the roads became rough, and the *springs* began to pitch the FAMILY COACH about. The *axles* groaned, the *linch-pins* became shaky, the *hubs* were in a pucker, the *spokes* gave a warning crack, and the *footman* woke up with a prodigious jerk, that nearly took his head off. The *coachman* now gathered up the *reins* and cracked the *whip* in earnest; the *old lady* squeaked, and told the *coachman* to be careful; the *coachman* got saucy, and said he knew his own business best; the *fat poodle* began to turn pale, and the *coach-dog* took precious good care to keep himself and his *tail* out of danger.

"But oh! ah! alas! the very next minute the FAMILY COACH went pounce into a great mud-hole. The *coachman* jumped off the *box*, the *footman* tumbled off the *foot-board*, and both tried to lift the *fore-wheels* and *hind-wheels*, but they found they couldn't do it. Then they got back to their places; the *coachman* cracked his *whip* tremendously; the *off-leader* and *near-leader*, *off-wheeler* and *near-wheeler*, bounced and jumped, and pranced and danced, till their *blinders* were twisted into their eyes; the *pole* rattled; the *reins* and *traces* creaked; both the *axles* groaned; but the *wheels* wouldn't turn.

"At last, slap, bang! with one tremendous crash! the *linch-pins* came out, and the *wheels* rolled off; the *two leaders* and *two wheelers* ran away with their *blinders;* the *lamps* were smashed; the *doors* and *windows* broken; the *fat poodle* fell on the *old lady;* the *old lady* tumbled down on the *floor*, which broke through, and all came pounce on the poor *coach-dog*, who lost his *tail* by its being squeezed off; and *coachman, footman, old lady, fat poodle,* and *coach-dog* lay all jumbled up amid

10

the ruins of *wheels, axles, reins, traces, whip, pole, lamps, foot-board, steps, windows, doors, linch-pins, hubs, spokes,* and *springs* which once composed that splendid old fossil, the FAMILY COACH."

There were lots of forfeits to redeem, notwithstanding the natural quickness of little Lucy and the dogs, cats, and monkeys to whirl and spring about. Of course you know that if you forget to turn around when your name is called, you must pay a forfeit. The redeeming of these made an immense deal of laughing and chattering. The dogs acted funny, the cats funnier, and the monkeys funniest of all; while little Lucy's eyes sparkled like diamonds, and she danced and sang the whole time; so, upon the whole, it was quite as delightful a party as one made altogether of good little boys and girls; for the best of all was, that not a single cross bark, snarl, mew, chatter, or squeal was heard; and I for one would much rather be invited to a party of perfectly polite and good-natured dogs, cats, and monkeys, than to one of children who wanted to slap and scratch. Wouldn't you?

———

"Oh you funny, funny Aunt Fanny!" cried the children, laughing heartily, "to make dogs and cats teach us politeness; who ever heard of such a thing before?"

"That's what *I* call pretty sharp shooting," said Fred.

"And the shot must have gone through and through you," observed Kitty, quietly. "You remember how you pulled my chair from under me just as I was going to sit upon it yesterday, and made me come down bang on the floor."

"Yes, and you shook the room so, I thought it would crack the looking-glass; and then you looked round so astonished and silly, I almost died laughing."

"Oh, Fred!" exclaimed Aunt Fanny;

"is it possible you were so rude? If I were an absolute monarch, I would condemn you to be upset once a day for a week in exactly the same manner. I am a great believer in the kind of punishment the boys call 'tit for tat.' If a boy should cut the string of your kite, I should cut the strings of *all* his kites for a whole season, explaining every time—'That's for punishment, my fine friend. I don't think you'll cut another boy's kite-string in a hurry.'"

Fred turned very red; but, standing up, he said pleasantly, "Here, Kitty, come and upset me."

She ran behind his chair, but he did not think she would play this trick before company, and he turned quickly, with such perfect confidence, as she snatched the chair away, that he came down with a most tremendous thump! which made the very windows rattle, amid the shouts and laughter of the rest.

"How do you like it?" asked Aunt Fanny, quietly.

"Not much," said Fred, grinning in rather a rueful manner. I'm cured, though. I don't think I shall upset anybody again ; and just let them try it on *me*—that's all."

At this they all laughed harder than ever, and declared that Aunt Fanny's rule for punishment was the very best they had ever heard of.

"But do you not see, my darlings," she said, seriously, "that it only proves the glorious wisdom of Our Saviour's golden rule? Whenever you are tempted to play a trick, or say a sharp thing, just stop one moment, and ask yourself, 'Would I like to have this done or said to *me?*' If you ask yourself this question *honestly*, the little monitor which God has placed in all your hearts, will answer you so faithfully and kindly, that you would be very naughty children not to listen to its whisperings.

"And now let me tell you the true de-

finition of politeness. It is '*real kindness
kindly expressed.*' Don't forget this. Put
this definition in *your* pop-guns, and fire
it off as often as you can, and, my word for
it, everybody you shoot will come to love
you dearly. For my part, I should like to
dine off such shots, red-hot, every day of
my life. And so good night, little Pop-gun
youngsters, and pleasant dreams to you
all."

"Ah, dear Aunt Fanny! please stay a
little minute longer," cried all the children, running to kiss her. "It's so very
early."

"Well, I believe I will stay just long
enough to ask your advice about something."

"Oh dear, yes! Ask away. We love
to give advice." And the six children
immediately tried to look as wise as twelve
large owls, or as Governor Wise of Vir-
ginia, who, they said, kept it all in his
name, and nowhere else; while Aunt

Fanny, with a very grave face, proceeded to observe—

"This story finishes the first volume of 'Pop-Guns.' Do you think it will do to go with 'Nightcaps' and the rest? or do you advise me to burn it up?"

"Burn it up!" screamed the children, running again to her and kissing her. "No, no, no; pray, don't. Have them printed, and we will read them twenty times, and play the 'Family Coach' too! Let's play Family Coach now."

And so they did; though, as there were only ten of them, Sophie had to be all the four horses, Kitty the coachman, footman, and old lady; while mamma, papa, Aunt Fanny, and the rest, were all sorts of things at once. But they had great fun, and were perfectly wornout with laughing, particularly when little Bob had to twirl round, which he always did in such a desperate hurry, that he tumbled over his own legs, and upset himself every time.

And, after that, the forfeits were enchanting; for Aunt Fanny knew a great many funny ones; and Fred said he *did* "*wish* Aunt Fanny was a 'real true child,' so they could have her to play with them the whole time;" which speech, she declared, was the very finest compliment she had ever received; and Uncle Fanny (that's Aunt Fanny's husband) said—

"Well, Peter, I always said you were about six months younger than either of your children, and now I am surer of it than ever."

"What makes Uncle Fanny call her 'Peter?'" whispered Kitty to Lou. "He always does it. He did it in one of the 'Mitten' books."

"Because he thinks it teases me," said Aunt Fanny, whose ears are very sharp, and heard the whisper.

"Why, Peteretta! *does* it tease you?" said Uncle Fanny.

"There! he is at it, worse than ever:

let's all go and shake him," cried Aunt
Fanny.

The six children rushed at him pell-mell
—and he got a splendid shaking—little
Bob squeezing one knee and tickling him
almost to death ; Peter the other, while the
rest of the children shook him just where
they could get at him.

" Ah ! he's sorry," cried Kitty, in a
sweet, coaxing voice; "hear how he
sighs !"

Sure enough, Uncle Fanny was sighing,
because he could not laugh any more, he
had got so weak ; but he caught at dear
little Kitty's comforting word, and gasped
out, " Oh yes, I'm sorry, dreadful sorry—
I'll never call Peter Aunt Fanny again—I
mean, Aunt Peter, Fannyretta—I mean—
oh, Peter ! ! I will be good !"

Aunt Fanny had given his ear a good
pinch, and the children laughed harder
than ever, to see him holding up his hands,
and pretending to be afraid of a little

woman about half his size, and they were just going to shake him again, when he ran for his life, and, getting out on the front stoop, declared he would not come into the house again.

So they had to let Aunt Fanny go to him, after she had promised not to be long before she fired off another pop-gun at them.

And they promised her to be always kind and good to their little companions, and make the very best use of their time —as Philip Wiseman did at last—and to "practise true politeness" everywhere, and towards everybody, like Beppo and his friends.

* * * * * * *

After Aunt Fanny went away, the children were so anxious to impress upon her mind the serious importance of having the first volume of Pop-guns printed immediately, that they called a mass meeting in the corner, before they bid their parents good-night.

"I say," said Fred, "let's write one of those things papa reads out of the paper, when any great man dies, beginning with, 'Whereas,' and going on with a whole lot of 'resolves' full of compliments."

"But I don't want Aunt Fanny to die," cried little Bob, beginning to rub his eyes.

"Oh no! She isn't going to die. But we don't want her to burn up our Pop-guns," explained Lou, kindly.

"Oh!" said Bob, and looked quite comforted.

So Fred got a sheet of paper, and filling a pen very full of ink, for fear it might dry up before he got it to the paper, he began to write; and by dint of breathing very hard, and bouncing up and down in his chair after finishing every sentence, he soon completed this elegant set of resolutions:—

"*Whereas*, As we are afraid Aunt Fanny may burn up Pop-guns, which would be awful; and

"*Whereas*, Ever so many children would be so sorry, they would not know what to do; therefore,

"*Resolved*, That the stories are perfectly delightful, and

would do the children more good than forty whippings, or a hundred doses of medicine; and

"*Resolved*, That after being told in the famous story of the "Dinner Party," that the

> Dogs and cats were so polite,
> They quite forgot to bark and bite,

it would never do to let all the rest of the children in the world lose a chance of growing as polite, as we mean to be after this, or as amiable and unselfish as Philip Badboy became; and so, dear Aunt Fanny, you will please to send your stories to Mr. Sheldon immediately, and ask him to get them printed in the very greatest hurry—real head-over-heels hurry, too."

"There !" cried Fred, reading the manifesto over with admiration, but with a vague idea that they did not sound quite right, particularly the last one. "There ! Now we must sign our names—ladies first."

So Sophie and the rest signed ; and Aunt Fanny got the resolutions before breakfast the next morning, and had a good laugh over them.

But she sent the stories to Mr. Sheldon, and here they are for her darlings out in the world.

The children to whom they were read have promised to make her happy by trying to profit by the good examples given, and avoid what is unlovely and sinful. Will *you* try too? Ah! tell Aunt Fanny that you will,—and that our Father in Heaven may help you, shall be her daily prayer.

ROLLO'S TOUR IN EUROPE.

BY JACOB ABBOTT,

Author of the " Rollo Books," " Florence Stories," " American Histories," &c., &c.

ORDER OF THE VOLUMES.

ROLLO ON THE ATLANTIC.

ROLLO IN PARIS.

ROLLO IN SWITZERLAND.

ROLLO IN LONDON.

ROLLO ON THE RHINE.

ROLLO IN SCOTLAND.

ROLLO IN GENEVA.

ROLLO IN HOLLAND.

ROLLO IN NAPLES.

ROLLO IN ROME.

Each volume fully illustrated.

Price per vol., **90** *cents.*

Mr. Abbott is the most successful writer of books for the young in this, or perhaps, any other country. " ROLLO'S TOUR IN EUROPE," is by far the greatest success of any of Mr. Abbott's works.

From the New York Observer.

"Mr. Abbott is known to be a pure, successful and useful writer for the young and old. He is also the most popular Author of juvenile books now living."

NEW JUVENILE BOOKS,

To be ready early in the coming Fall.

A NEW SERIES BY AUNT FANNY,

Author of "Nightcap," "Mitten," and "Pet Books."

THE POP-GUN STORIES.

In 6 vols. 16mo., beautifully illustrated.

I.—POP-GUNS.
II.—ONE BIG POP-GUN.
III.—ALL SORTS OF POP-GUNS.
IV.—FUNNY POP-GUNS.
V.—GRASSHOPPER POP-GUNS.
VI.—POST-OFFICE POP-GUNS.

Aunt Fanny is one of the most successful writers for children in this country, as is attested by the very wide sale her previous books have had, and we feel sure that the mere announcement of this new series will attract the attention of her host of admirers.

A NEW SERIES BY T. S. ARTHUR,

Author of "Household Library," and "Arthur's Juvenile Library."

HOME STORIES.

3 vols., 16mo., fully illustrated.

LIST OF VOLUMES.

HIDDEN WINGS.
SOWING THE WIND.
SUNSHINE AT HOME.

The name of this Author is a sufficient Guarantee of the excellence of the Series.

www.ingramcontent.com/pod-product-compliance
Lightning Source LLC
Chambersburg PA
CBHW020009030726
47500CB00002B/503